DROUGHT

By Teresa Meyerhoeffer Christensen

Original cover created by
Chelsea Christensen Buttars

ISBN- 13: 9781732880238

ISBN- 10: 1732880239

Bridge2WorldsBooks
5942 Harvest Point Circle
Mountain Green, Utah 84050

www.TeresaMeyerhoefferChristensen.com

Dedicated to
those on the autism spectrum
and others who love someone that is.

Other books by this author:

Hijacking Happiness (non-fiction)

There is Love

Not Really Homeless

Seth Row

Angels Unshelved

Preface:
Water or the lack of water which we call Drought:

drought
/drout/
Noun

1: a period of dryness especially when prolonged, specifically: one that causes extensive damage to crops or prevents their successful growth.
2: a prolonged or chronic shortage or lack of something expected or desired.

The four types of drought are meteorological (lack of precipitation), agricultural (lack of moisture in the soil), hydrological (low levels of water in lakes and reservoirs) and socio-economical (water shortages in drinking and running water).

Water covers 71% of the earth's surface. There are approximately 326 million cubic miles of water on the planet. In actuality, that amounts to an average of 84 million liters (2.2 million gallons) for each person on earth. However, only 0.5% of the earth's water is available freshwater. 97% of the earth's water (320 million cubic gallons) is found in oceans and is too salty for drinking, growing crops, and for most industrial uses except cooling. 3% of the earth's water is fresh, but 2.5% is unavailable due to being locked up in glaciers, polar ice caps, the atmosphere or the soil. The rest of the unavailable freshwater supply is either highly polluted or lies too far beneath the surface of the earth to extract at an affordable cost. This water supply is continually collected, purified, and redistributed in the natural hydrologic (water) cycle. In more manageable ratios, if the world's water supply were only 100 liters (24 gallons), our usable water supply of freshwater would be about 0.003 liters (one-half teaspoon) per person.

The main sources of freshwater are: 1) Groundwater or water which infiltrates into the ground through porous materials and goes deeper into the earth. It fills pores and fractures in layers of underground rock called aquifers. Some of this water lies too far under the earth's surface to be extracted at an affordable cost. 2) Surface-water runoff or precipitation that does not infiltrate into the ground or return to the atmosphere, in streams, rivers, lakes, wetlands, and reservoirs. 3) Snow that is 4 inches (10 cm) deep contains about the same amount of water as 1/3 inch (1 cm) of rain.

The breakdown of percentages of water found on earth are 97.2% is found in oceans, 2.0% in ice caps or glaciers, 0.62% in groundwater (but not all can be accessed), 0.009% in freshwater lakes, 0.008% in inland seas or salt lakes, 0.001% in the atmosphere, and 0.0001% in rivers.

Water use in the U.S. is divided with 8% used domestically, 33% going to agricultural use, and 59% used in industry. Over 600 gallons per day per person is being diverted for farm irrigation and livestock use from natural aquatic sources. More than half of the people in the U.S. get their water from groundwater.

Approximate home water usage measured by gallons include: shaving and allowing the faucet to run (3), flushing a toilet (1.6-5), brushing your teeth with faucet running (5), cooking three meals (8), cleaning the house (8), washing dishes for three meals (10), washing clothes (20-30), washing dishes with faucet running (30), watering lawn (30-40), washing car (30-40), taking a bath (30-40), and 8-minute shower (40 or about 5 gallons/minute).

Americans use about 1/3 more water in the summer than the rest of the year due to watering lawns. There are about 10 million acres of lawn in the U.S., which requires 270 billion gallons of water every week. That's enough to give every person in the world a shower for four days in a row. Most lawns only need an inch of water each week.

A leak that fills up a coffee cup in 10 minutes will waste over 3,000 gallons of water in a year. That's 65 glasses of water every day for a year. A leaky toilet can waste over

22,000 gallons of water in one year; enough to take three baths every day.

The effects of drought on the environment include: 1) wetlands dry up, 2) pollution of surface water, 3) the health of plants are adversely impacted, 4) dust storms become common, 5) loss of biodiversity, 6) wildfires become common, 7) animals are forced to migrate, 8) increased desertification, and 9) famines around the world.

Chapter 1 - India 1876

Anoop

"Drought is a slow-motion disaster –
it's a slow and creeping death for plant and animal life..."
-Kenneth Dierschke

Anoop kept his head dipped below the nearly four-foot-tall jowar leaves encircling the cleared patch of earth as he reverently moved between the five small mounds. He did not view this detour as the shirking of his duties but as a necessary daily homage. He was not sure his baba would feel the same. The names Viti Hope, Pia Grace, Devya Joy, Zahira Faith, and Reyansh John were carved onto wooden crosspieces perpendicularly bound with jute strands to thick branches forming five makeshift crosses. The crudely hewn symbols of everlasting life adorned one end of each earthen hill. Anoop lay down on the parched ground between Zahira and Reyansh shielding his eyes from the hot sun and wondered for the millionth time why his name was not etched here amid the others.

The jowar plants waved in the wind their flapping sound soothing him. Perhaps this was what it felt like to be at sea with water rolling all around. Anoop would likely never know or ever see that much water all in one place. Water was at a premium here. The thirsty jowar crop was too thin and too short this year, just like the people in their area. Even children did not grow well in India, the reminder of that fact lay still and silent beside him.

In the distance he heard a voice calling. His ma probably had their midday meal of roti, rice, and dal ready. He had eaten the same for breakfast and would for dinner as well. With the impending sparse harvest, there would likely be only two meals a day this winter, so he did not want to miss one now. Anoop pushed himself upward and said goodbye to his planted siblings wondering where they were and what they were doing in the next life.

The ocean of yellowing leaves with red heads parted before him as he passed. His ma had told him that jowar was called sorghum where her family came from and the plants looked like a smaller version of tasseled corn when growing. They would harvest the crop soon to be traded for other items that they needed or grind it into flour to make their flatbread.

Some people used it to feed their cows, but the Sharma's did not own a cow. Maybe if they did the brahma would bring luck to their land.

Their family also grew a much smaller crop of turmeric. The spice root took much longer to grow but was more valuable and added security for their family to survive during bad jowar years. This year their small area of turmeric did not look promising either. His baba Mehul had not smiled in a week. The weight of the slim harvest must be pressing down the sides of his lips.

Anoop pushed through the fabric door that covered the opening to their two-room dwelling. The dirt floor had been brushed clean and the ladder which led to the loft where he slept leaned against a sidewall. Ma greeted him with her bright jade eyes that always seemed happy to see him. Her golden-brown hair was pulled back and pinned up in a pile on her head but was not covered like many of the other Indian women. His ma was not really from India even though she was born here. She looked different, so Anoop looked a little different too. His eyes were a mixture of both his parents'. His baba's dark dirt-brown eyes and his ma's spring-grass green ones mixed to create a color ma called hazel with golden sparkles tossed in too. Anoop liked his uniqueness, his eyes reflected the colors of the earth's bounty, but he knew the differences made his ma's life harder here.

Ma looked the same as the other women of the village from the neck down. Yards of brightly colored cotton cloth wrapped around her waist with one end draped over a shoulder, the arm protruding from her sari set their midday meal on the wooden plank table. The gently spiced sauce emitted a tantalizing smell that called for Anoop to dip into it with the flatbread. His ma created magical tastes with minimal spices. He bet she could make even an old jowar leaf taste good. But Anoop respectfully waited for his baba to sit and begin before taking his own portion.

Mehul arrived looking hot and tired with perspiration beading up on his forehead below his turban. Anoop wondered if the turban kept the sun and heat off of his baba or made him warmer. He would find out for himself in a few more years when he became old enough to be required to wear the turban too, if he decided to wear one at all. His religious experience was as much a mash-up as his eyes. His baba was Sikh, a sect of the Hindu faith, and ma's dadi or grandfather had arrived in India as a Christian missionary. Their family practiced both religions and sometimes Anoop got mixed up as to which belief was which.

Baba began eating so Anoop scooped up a helping of the pungent dal on his roti and took a hungry bite. Looking up he saw his mother sit and bow her head silently over her meager portion before she partook. A touch of shame flamed across Anoop's face and he wished he had waited to thank his ma's God before he had filled his belly. Baba did not seem to notice.

"Where'd you disappear off to this morning, beta?" Mehul's words floated out of his mouth on heatwaves between his bites of food. "It looks like we will be harvesting our crop early this season. The dry earth cannot give us more growth. I will need your help."

Ma protectively answered baba before Anoop could reply, "He is still just a child Mehul. Perhaps you could get some of our neighbors to trade time with you and help carry the load?" Anoop was the only child she had left to tend to, so the devoted attention he received was multiplied many times.

"Hiya, you'll make the child soft. He needs to learn to work." Baba called ma Hiya, even though her birth name was Briary, because he said she had stolen a piece of his heart from the first time he had set eyes on her.

"His back will be bent from toiling over these fields long before we leave this world. I just hope our son can capture some moments of youthful joy before the weight of life presses down on him too." Ma spoke softly.

Anoop had not had to say a word. He did not feel soft and he liked to help his baba, but he also felt a daily pull to visit his deceased siblings. The time he spent there amid their mounds filled him in a way that made him better at whatever else he did that day. He was the only one left to carry out all of their combined dreams and any achievements that they might have made. Anoop knew he had nothing very special to offer, but he hoped to do something wonderful to make up for the lives in this family that had been cut short and would no longer be lived. After this meal, he would follow his father out into the fields without distraction or complaint.

Chapter 1 notes: Jowar (a noun pronounced "joe-were" in English) is a variety of sorghum extensively cultivated in Asia and Africa that is used to make flatbreads. Jowar is globally being touted as the "new quinoa" for its gluten-free, whole grain goodness.

Chapter 2 – Oregon 2020

Juniper

"It's so dry the trees are bribing the dogs."
- Charles Martin, Chasing Fireflies: A Novel of Discovery

Juniper felt the furry pint-sized face with cool wet nose nuzzle under her chin. She should be a more professional volunteer, but puppy-dog eyes, literally, not the pale comparison on humans, dropped her defenses every time. Besides, these rejected canines needed the extra loving, didn't everyone really. Puppies were not often deposited at the rescue, but this week they had received a whole litter of what looked like some kind of terrier and shaggy dog mix, better known as mongrels. Mutts were always her favorites anyway, who knew what hidden potential was stashed inside their DNA or who they would eventually become.

Juniper was in the process of naming the six pups, even though the shelter workers were repeatedly cautioned not to. The rule had been established "for their own benefit" the supervisor said, to prevent them from getting too attached. Too late, Juniper formed an attachment to almost every beast the moment she witnessed their pathetic circumstances upon arrival and looked into their vacillating-between-frightened-and-trusting eyes.

Princess Prada was the only exception. Juniper had named her but was not sad to see her go. The Afghan hound always seemed to think she was somehow above all of the other dogs as well as any of the workers. It looked almost as if she held her nose in the air when she pranced lightly on tiptoes among the kennel dwellers seeming to avoid any contact with the lesser beings there. But the female dog, literally a bitch, was beautiful in a prissy way and had rapidly found a new home.

Soccer Momma was one of Juniper's all-time favorites. The old boxer German Shepard mix had arrived at their doorstep with a greying muzzle and had never found a home outside of the kennel. However, the aged dog had created one here amid all the other breeds and human workers. Soccer Momma nurtured every other dog who came in and seemed to know when any of the staffers needed extra tenderness as well. She was special, gifted with dog-dar...a canine emotional radar. Juniper was glad that Soccer Momma's last year was a loved one in her non-kill kennel home. Juniper could never work in a place that put dogs down. She shuttered at the thought.

Juniper's long brown braids hung over each ear past her shoulders, sort of like basset hound ears she thought. Her big brown eyes projected a hound dog look as well. She definitely felt more comfortable with this pack of pups than with people most days.

The new puppy nipped playfully at her fingers with his pokey-sharp baby teeth. "What should I name you little one? Jaws doesn't quite fit...let's see..." The puppy's paws reached for Juniper's braids in a circular motion wanting to play. "That's it, you are hereby dubbed Dr. Strange and the rest of your litter will be the other Avengers...the tough guy is definitely Iron Man, your handsome brother will be Thor, how about Hulk for the biggest boy and your sisters can be Black Widow and this last little girl Marvel, without the Captain." Dr. Strange continued to paw at Juniper, then licked her chin as if in approval.

Stetson Buttars called down the corridor to Juniper as he ambled towards her between the two rows of kennels, "Juniper, it looks like our newest recruits have received enough attention from you for the moment, could you clean out the rest of the kennels in this section and make sure all the bowls have fresh water before you go?"

17

"Sure-thing Stetson, I was just finishing up with the pups," Juniper replied as she set Dr. Strange down with the other Avengers. It seemed like an appropriate name for the group. They certainly had reason to avenge being dumped off on the side of the road in a cardboard box. Some people did not deserve to be pet owners. The Cretans must have had better options somewhere in their empty heads that they were either unable or unwilling to decipher and carry out.

Stetson's lanky body stopped and bent over the rambunctious sextuplets. He was a good volunteer manager, even though not much older than Juniper, and he was definitely cute. The natural kind of cute that took no effort on his part. Not that Juniper really noticed. He wore slim fit jeans and a gray t-shirt sporting a band logo that Juniper was not familiar with. She thought cowboy boots would better fit with his name, but Stetson was wearing high-top black sneakers. His dark shaggy hair was brushed back from his violet eyes and stubbly whiskers were attempting to sprout on his upper lip and chin. Juniper still found the pups cuter, but he wasn't bad. Stetson had a rapport with the dogs but was not a bleeding heart like Juniper, so he added objectivity. He was as willing to scoop out poop as he was to give a vaccine or even to write up the managerial paperwork. Juniper enjoyed the team of decent human beings she worked with here after school at the

All Dogs Go to Heaven…Just Not Yet Rescue. Helping rescue the dogs was refreshing since she hadn't been able to do much in the way of rescuing her own family.

Juniper had moved to Oregon with her mother and twin brother six years ago when she was nine. Her father still lived in New York City, most of the time, working on Wall Street in the financial district. Her mom had decided to find a better school and location for her brother "to thrive in." Conifer was obsessed with nature, botany, horticulture, almost anything green. He was pretty much a genius and a walking google.com when it came to anything that grew…in the plant world anyway. There wasn't much that grew in NYC's cement, so relocation was deemed necessary by their mother.

Conifer's skills did not extend to other growing things, like animals or especially people. He had been diagnosed as "on the spectrum." Besides encyclopedic knowledge of the plant world, about the only other words Conifer shared were usually in the form of a repeated song lyric or occasional quote from some of the literature he read. It was like those borrowed words were somehow safer since they had been composed by someone else. He was not comfortable sharing his own words - perhaps he found them too personal? Juniper was not really sure. She just knew she loved her contrastingly colored, blond,

19

blue-eyed brother and his unique world. Yet, she had to admit it was easier to not go to the same school with him anymore.

When they had attended school together, Juniper was her twin's self-assigned protector. She regretted not being able to fulfill that role at his new school, but she was often protecting Conifer from slights that he did not even comprehend were insults anyway. He didn't really care, so why did she care so very deeply? Now she was able to avoid the hurt she absorbed for him. Hopefully, the students were nicer to Conifer at Oak Leaf Academy. Everyone at his new school was also on some level of the spectrum. Perhaps they understood each other's alternate worlds better than she did or at least were not offended when they didn't.

The kennels were de-dunged and filled with fresh water, the puppies each given one last snuggle and Stetson reported to before Juniper exited out the glass front door. She wasn't really ready to go home, but there were things she needed to do there, and Conifer's bus would drop him off shortly. Juniper began the nearly two-mile trek home. She liked walking, it cleared her head and she didn't have to wait for her mother to pick her up since Juniper didn't have her driver's license yet. Juniper wondered if driving was another thing Conifer may not be allowed to do.

The twins had both been named for evergreen trees, but that was where the similarity ended. They were diametrically opposite in everything else. He was a boy; she was a girl. He was fair; she was dark. He was not tall for a boy his age; she was lanky and willowy long. He was autisticly non-social and she needed human or at least animal connection. He was a genius - in things that interested him, maybe more a savant - and she had to work to understand most subjects, except dogs, they came easy for her. Perhaps she had developed skills when dealing with a non-verbal brother that translated to the animal realm. Conifer was never called Con. He was far too literal for any kind of con, the name didn't fit, and he wouldn't answer to it anyway. She may get away with Conniff occasionally but rarely tried. Her brother taught her a ton. He was truly her other and probably better half. The opposite half that balanced her out and grounded her on a daily basis.

Their mother Brooke was a good mom. She just divided herself a bit lopsidedly. Sixty percent of her time was spent dealing with Conifer's things. Thirty percent was split between her volunteer commitments ("that a wealthy stay-at-home wife was expected to do") and taking care of her own personal needs. The last ten percent, or less, that was left-over went to Juniper. Juniper understood, she got it, but at times it sucked. Names were on Juniper's mind today... take out one of the "*O*'s" in her mother's name and she would be *broke*, not *Brooke*. Her mom had enough to deal with and was just one *O* away from broken, so Juniper was always *O*-kay no matter what, to prevent the loss of her mother's second *O*.

Juniper beat the bus home on foot, but her mom was already there after all.

"Welcome home Junie, how was school and how were the dogs today?" Brooke with both *O*'s asked as she gave her daughter a quick hug.

"Both were doable. No grades below a B today and a litter of six pups deserted roadside were dropped off at the rescue." Juniper shared as she headed for a snack.

"That day sounds more than doable to me. Good grades and a pack of puppies are awesome I would say," her mother responded cheerleader-like.

"Hey mom, can you take me to get my driver's permit? I have to have a permit for at least six months to practice driving before I can even apply to take the driver's test and get my license. Oregon isn't like New York City where you have to be eighteen to drive." Juniper did a quick subject change to squeeze in her needs before Conifer got home.

"Let me look over my calendar and hopefully we can make that happen," her mom replied as Conifer walked through the door. Too late, their brief conversation would now be put on pause, not to be resumed until an indeterminant time in the future.

Chapter 3 - India 1876

Briary

"Blessed is the man (woman) that trusts in the Lord, and whose hope is in Him. For he (she) will be like a tree planted by the water that spreads out their roots by the river. They do not fear when the heat comes, but their leaves will be green; they never worry in a year of drought, and never fail to bear fruit." - Jeremiah 17:7-8

Briary Fountain Sharma was not aware of the fact that she was a beautiful woman. Her fine features, even powdered in dust and draped in poverty chic, were undeniably lovely. She cleared away the empty platter and bowl and began to wipe them clean using minimal water. There was not enough water to waste on extra rinses. Briary had given up the tradition of using utensils to eat, except on special occasions, so there was not much dishware to wash after each meal. The Sharma's partook of their meals from shared serving bowls. Briary completed the dishwashing with conscious love as she did each mundane task in her life. She found joy in feeding her family and tending to their simple needs.

When she was a young girl living in the mission, Briary would never have imagined herself one day becoming the wife of an Indian farmer. Life brought the unexpected, but the unexpected was not necessarily bad. A person could survive and serve in various capacities wherever they landed. No, it wasn't the circumstances of her existence, but the devastating losses that were taking a toll on her and making her old before her time. She felt her first loss, that of her mother, acutely these days. She could use the advice of an older, wiser woman but instead sought comfort and solace in the teachings of her youth.

Her Grandfather John Fountain had been one of the first Christian missionaries to India in the early 1800s. He arrived in Midnapore and began teaching school there. Because the East India Company was hostile to the missionaries, they had settled in the Danish colony at Serampore. The community of missionaries and teachers were joined by a man named William Carey who founded a university there. Grandpa John's wife had not taken to the new country and returned to Great Britain with her younger children leaving her oldest son Tristan with his father in India. Briary's life would have been much different if her father had gone back to England with his mother. Or maybe she would not have been born at all. She was not sure how that worked in the eternal scheme of things.

Her father was not missionary-minded and did not fit in well with the religious lifestyle. He had a more rebellious nature. Tristan found an opportunity in the British East India Trading Company with Robert Clive who led the company with military prowess. Clive eventually conquered India into submission for Great Britain. Where her grandfather had been a lover, her father was a fighter. Briary assumed her father must have at least loved her mother. She knew very little about the woman who bore her, beyond the fact that she was an English woman who died giving birth to Briary. An ironic twist of fate…her mother died giving birth to her and her children died after she gave birth to them - all except Anoop. She was the bringer of death or a link to it on both ends of the equation.

Father Tristan had not known what to do with a "squalling baby girl" as he put it. So, he had taken Briary back to be raised in the mission by those that worked and taught with Grandpa John. That was the one blessing her father had given her - secure, faith-centered surroundings to be raised in. If her grandfather were still alive Briary may still be living there with him, but after he passed, she had gone off to serve in one of the outlying missions. She wondered at times why he had not sent her back to Great Britain. She supposed she could have gone herself when he died, but India was all she knew. It was her home. Even though not all who looked upon her saw it that way. They saw the British woman she had never been.

Perhaps resentment stemmed from the fact that many in India missed the power and imposing illusion of security they felt during the over three-hundred-year reign of the conquering Mughal empire. Some saw her as a part of the English usurpers. Her father may have been involved in the takeover, but on the inside, Briary was one of the natives, even if her outside didn't reflect it. Besides, wasn't British rule better for the country anyway? With Queen Victoria now the proclaimed Empress of India, there was far less brutality. The practice of *suttee* where Indian widows were required to throw themselves on the funeral pyre of their husbands when they died had been abolished. Hindu widows were now even allowed to remarry. The new British rule had gotten rid of the dacoits, thugs, and other such pests of Indian society and provided charitable aid in time of famine. Infanticide had been banned. Briary could not imagine how a mother could consider killing her child in the first place? She still grieved daily over the deaths of each of her children.

Change was often hard, but it could be a blessing. Different was not always bad, just different. Some things at the mission had been better and some things were better now in her house and life she had created with Mehul. The most difficult part of living here was not the drought on the land, but the drought in her heart. It was remembering and catching glimpses of Viti, Pia, Devya, Zahira, and Reyansh everywhere she looked. Briary would startle, still thinking she saw one of them at times. Their presences were everywhere. In reality, she would not want to live anywhere else…anywhere else where her deceased children may not be lingering near. She had given each child a faith-filled middle name- Hope, Grace, Joy, Faith and Reyansh's after his great-grandpa John - but the names had not helped them survive.

Maybe their deaths were her curse for marrying outside her faith and causing Mehul to be disowned by most of his family. But how could that be right in the eyes of any God? Mehul may not be a man of many words, but his heavily accented English, intense black eyes and warm white-toothed smile had captured her heart. The humble man was goodness personified and he had given up much more than she had with their union. She may have given up her way of life, but he gave up his family. Briary still lived the beliefs she had been raised by and she did not believe that loving someone so fiercely could be wrong. Hopefully someday other Sharma hearts would soften to accept their English daughter-in-law. Regardless, she was grateful for the man she had married.

Briary could not remember a day that Mehul had not greeted her with absolute love and appreciation. At least once a week she found a flower of some variety laying on their bed or on the table for her. She had no idea where Mehul picked them, perhaps growing wild in some secluded patch, they were not from anywhere on their farm. If he didn't have a blossom for her, Mehul would recite a line of poetry or use his own words to pay her a compliment for an attribute she often did not even know that she possessed. He saw her through eyes of love, thus making the image of herself that he reflected back to her appear more lovely than in reality she knew she was. The simple acts she performed in their household were even magnified by his gratitude. Earlier in their marriage, the moment he walked through the door at the end of his long physically exhausting days, he would lift her off the floor and swing her around proclaiming he was the luckiest man in India or on the whole planet. Briary could never regret her decision to bind her life and future to this giving man. He truly treasured her.

The worst part of their union was not knowing why her children were gone so soon. Her babies were born pink and healthy with a strong cry, but they had not thrived like other children in the village. All five ate well, but the food did not help them grow tall or stout. They seemed to get winded easily at play and tasted of salt when she kissed them. It was as if an unquenchable thirst had driven them to drink unattainable ocean water and the saltine crystals had remained behind on their skin. Coughs came easily and lasted long. The doctor she had taken them to in Agra had no idea how to heal her children. He sent them away with herbs that did not make them well or help them breathe any easier. One by one each had died in her arms struggling to get air through thick phlegm, drowning in their own body fluids. Sweet fragile Devya had been barely two. Only Anoop had survived past eight years of age. It appeared he had apparently avoided the curse.

Her cherished boy blew her a kiss as he headed out to assist his father in his efforts to eke a crop out of their dry land. Anoop's eyes connected with hers briefly; the boy was observant for his young age. "Ma are you alright? Do you need me to stay?"

"I am well. Go with your baba, he needs you more." Briary focused on the son in front of her and willed the tears for the ones that were no longer here to stay behind her eye-lashed lids.

Chapter 3 notes: the historical facts about John Fountain, William Carey, and the British East India Trading Company led by Robert Clive are all true, as well as the information about the changes in India's society under British rule. However, Tristan and Briary Fountain and their descendants are all fictional characters.

Chapter 4 – Oregon 2020

Brooke

*"Waiting for you is like waiting for rain in this
drought...useless and disappointing."*
-A Cinderella Story

"How was your day at school today Conifer?" Brooke asked keeping the question as clear and direct as possible while attempting to make eye contact as her son walked through the door into their living room.

Conifer acknowledged his mother with a brief glance and then replied in monotone to no one in general, "*Made to feel the way that every child should sit and listen, sit and listen. Went to school and I was very nervous. No one knew me, no one knew me. Hello teacher tell me what's my lesson. Look right through me, look right through me.*"

Brooke was not exactly sure what her son meant, but responded, "I am sure your teachers know who you are, and know that you are there, and are glad you are there too. You are such a smart boy." She wanted to give him a hug but did not want to make him uncomfortable or run him off to his bedroom just yet. Maybe she could get more clarification.

"It is from the song *Mad World*, Mom. Pretty great song actually, maybe a little haunting, but a classic." Juniper educated her mother.

"Well, I will have to look up that song for sure. Anything else I should know? Did you learn anything new? Or how was the bus ride home?" Brooke pressed.

"*I used to get mad at my school. The teachers who taught me weren't cool. You're holding me down, turning me round, filling me up with your rules…. Don't want to be taught to be no fool. Rock, rock, rock, rock, rock 'n' roll high school… On a bus stop in the town we rule the school… And that's what I learned in school today. That's what I learned in school.*" Conifer awkwardly rapped out his answers. Brooke turned to her daughter bewildered. Juniper had a much vaster knowledge of pop song lyrics than she did and played interpreter at times.

"That is a medley of three or four songs about school mashed together, I think. I caught The Beatles, the Ramones and maybe Seeger?" Juniper shrugged. "You got me on the other one."

Conifer already disinterested with the conversation sat down and pulled his Earth Science textbook out of his canvas backpack and began thumbing through it. Brooke cupped the top of his wavy blonde head in her hands and gave it a quick kiss. This less confining embrace usually didn't agitate him. She could no longer reach the top of his head when he was standing since her teenage son had recently passed her in height. He was definitely done communicating and Juniper had exited the premises, so Brooke was left with her own thoughts as she watched Conifer calmly absorb information.

It had been the best decision to bring him to Oak Leaf Academy. In New York City he had been totally non-verbal and did not engage in his surroundings at all. Conifer had never been violent, but he was more at peace in this less stimulating environment. At first, Blaze had put up a fight to keep them all in New York when she had proposed moving out west for Conifer to attend a school specialized in his diagnosis and interests. He now seemed to be relieved by the arrangement. His "autistic son" cramped his style. Brooke hated it when Blaze defined Conifer by his diagnosis. He was not her autistic son, but her son who happened to have autism. She had originally been concerned about giving birth to a child with cystic fibrosis since the gene ran in her family. They had dodged that bullet but were hit with autism instead. At least

Conifer was healthy. He had so much potential and would hopefully lead a long fulfilling life.

At first Blaze flew out every weekend. He was still working on Wall Street and it was disruptive emotionally for Conifer to travel back and forth. Luckily, the Ridgeways had the money to finance travel and it kept them a family. After a few months, the trips home went to every other week, then to once a month and now, six years later, Blaze came home once a quarter if that. The sad thing was none of them really cared if he was around. Life was less stressful with him gone. Brooke had just finished reading *The Psychopath Test: A Journey Through the Madness Industry* by British author Jon Ronson and was starting to fear that her husband may be afflicted with the mindset. Blaze manifested over half of the symptoms on the twenty-point checklist. There was something off in the man. He was charming enough, but there was a superficial void. At forty-one she could see many red flags that she had missed in her twenties.

Brooke met Blaze after one of her shows. He was waiting for her outside the Ambassador Theater after watching her in the chorus of *Chicago*. He offered to take her out for a late-night quiet dinner or to a club if she preferred. He was older than she was by at least ten years but looked so strikingly handsome and important in his fitted black suit with a crisp white shirt and skinny black tie. His colorless eyes had pierced her, and she hadn't the power to say no to the man. That night began a whirlwind courtship, she was not sure she could call it a romance, but it was intense and captivating.

On Wednesday nights when *Chicago* was dark, Brooke was off. So, on Wednesdays, or on other nights when Blaze could convince her to use an understudy, he would whisk her away to the opera, or fly her to a dinner in some exotic location. Once they even landed in Paris for only eight hours. She was literally living the jet-setter lifestyle and barely had time to breathe. It hadn't bothered her that they never went out with other couples or to visit their families; he kept Brooke all to himself. Blaze swept her off her feet and he definitely used the right broom.

Less than a year from the night they met, the couple had a small ceremony at the Trinity Church located in New York City's Financial District. That should have given her a clue where his heart truly dwelt, but it was a lovely affair with just a few of her family members and a couple of close friends. After a honeymoon to Fiji, she moved into his brownstone in Manhattan just a few blocks away from where he worked. They were the ultimate New York power couple combining both the business and theater worlds of the Big Apple. Before long Blaze started to complain that her work infringed upon their nightlife in the city and that he needed her with him at business dinners to help impress clients. She gave up a few nights a week to be with Blaze, but she loved the stage and did not quit performing until she became pregnant with the twins at twenty-five.

Even after Juniper and Conifer were born, she was still able to keep up with life in the city. They hired a full-time nanny to make it all work. She was no longer in the chorus of *Chicago* or *The Scarlet Pimpernel*, but there were charity dinners and nights out where Brooke was always the dutiful dazzling wife on Blazes' arm. She was the yin to his yang…her *brook* never extinguished his *blaze*, but his fire absorbed her water. They struggled to find balance as a couple.

By the time the twins were two, their toddlers' differences were becoming obvious. Not only was their coloring opposite ends of the spectrum, so were their social interactions. Juniper was starting to babble and say actual words. She smiled and liked the attention. Whereas Conifer was totally silent and preferred to be alone making very little eye contact with any of them. The boy just liked to stare at their house plants as if watching them grow. Brooke knew girls usually talked earlier than boys, but there was something more going on here. After extensive testing, the verdict was autism, non-verbal, but highly functioning. Today the medical world calls it being "on the spectrum". Blaze was not really devastated. He just ignored the diagnosis like it didn't really happen. But as Conifer grew it became more and more impossible to ignore.

Brooke's new focus became finding the best treatments and programs for her son. She eventually realized that he needed to be away from the pavement and able to plant and watch things sprout in the soil. When the twins were nine, they moved so Conifer could participate in a nature-based program at Oak Leaf Academy where they "helped those on the spectrum grow as tall and strong as an oak tree physically, mentally and emotionally". It was a perfect fit for Conifer, and Juniper was easy enough to adapt anywhere. Now Conifer spent his days immersed in a positive program that gave him identity, purpose and he was growing a gigantic garden out back. He even communicated verbally with them when he was at home, albeit understanding his lyrical responses could be complicated at times. It would be helpful if Conifer used more Broadway tunes for his dialog, Brooke would have had a better chance at picking up on his points of conversation.

Brooke slipped the headphones from Conifer's ears to rest around his neck and sat next to her silent son who was totally engrossed in his schoolbook. She could sense whatever he was studying was something he was excited about even if the young man never expressed much emotion. Her eyes searched the page that was open and saw pictures with descriptions of various evergreen trees including both juniper and conifer varieties. Conifer looked up at his mother with a meaningful light in his eyes.

"That is pretty cool Conifer. You will have to let me know all that you learn about you and your sister's namesakes. Or we can read it together," Brooke suggested. "And after that let's go check out the garden. How does that sound?" Anything that formed a connection or bond between them was outstanding.

Her boy who would shortly become a man nodded and began reading in his robotic voice the classifications and information about the trees that gave color and life to his world.

Chapter 4 notes: The Twenty-point Hare PCL-R Checklist for Psychopaths includes…1) Glibness/superficial charm 2) Grandiose sense of self-worth 3) Need for stimulation/proneness to boredom 4) Pathological lying 5) Conning/manipulation 6) Lack of remorse or guilt 7) Shallow affect 8) Callous/lack of empathy 9) Parasitic lifestyle 10) Poor behavior controls 11) Promiscuous sexual behavior 12) Early behavior problems 13) Lack of realistic long-term goals 14) Impulsivity 15) Irresponsibility 16) Failure to accept responsibility for own actions 17) Many short-term marital relationships 18) Juvenile delinquency 19) Revocation of conditional release 20) Criminal versatility.

Song lyrics Conifer spoke- *Mad World*, by Roland Orzabal. *Getting Better* by The Beatles. *Rock 'N' Roll High School* by Ramones. *We Rule the School* by Belle and Sebastian. *What Did You Learn in School Today?* by Pete Seeger

Chapter 5 – India 1876

Mehul

(Hindi: मेहुल) is an Indian male given name of
Sanskrit origin, meaning *rain* or *cloud*.

*"It was raining on a drought field, not from the sky,
it was raining from the farmer's eye. – Man*

Mehul's sandal-clad toe kicked at the hard-packed
dirt. The ground did not seem to hold any moisture. The dry
farmer feared if he did not harvest what crop he had now, the
stunted jowar would shrivel away and there would be nothing
left of value for him to harvest in a few more weeks. An
immature crop would be better than none all at. Training
Anoop wasn't the same as having an adult man to assist him,
but Mehul could not afford to pay or trade for help this year.
They would make very little (if any) profit as it was and Mehul
had worked in his own father's fields even before he was eight
years old. Anoop could be a good worker when given a

specific task, the boy was just easily distracted. The scythe was too heavy and awkward for a child to swing, and his Hiya would not be happy if he had Anoop do anything that looked dangerous, but their beta could follow behind and gather the swathed crop to put into bundles for transport to market.

Mehul was a poor man, but happy for the most part despite their meager existence. He felt blessed to have any property at all to sustain his family. The land he worked as a child was his father's land, this land he now toiled over was not the land that he had planted, harvested and learned the farmer's trade on many years ago. His father's land went to his brothers. Not because they were older, but because they had married brides of the same faith in marriages arranged by his parents. Their different castes did not matter as the Sikh, unlike the Hindus, believed that all were equal in God's eyes. All Sikh or Hindu at least Mehul now realized, his bride had been neither.

Mehul had intended to marry the bride arranged for him. He was not a disobedient son and he was sure that the Indian girl chosen for him would have been a dutiful wife. It had nothing to do with his intended's appearance either as he had never set eyes on his selected bride. The girl lived in a village a half-day away and the circumstances had all been arranged by both sets of parents when Mehul was still young.

However, he had not expected to have his heart betray him by emphatically choosing a different bride. If he had not chosen Briary, he would no longer have been able to breathe. It was that simple, she was his life.

On one of his father's requested trips to town when he was just outside of Agra on the road to Delhi, he passed the Gurudwara Guru Ka Taal temple as he did on each journey. The structure was a beautiful sprawling center of Sikh worship built over an area that had previously been a taal or reservoir. It had been built in the 1600s to collect and conserve rainwater in Agra. The water of the reservoir was used for irrigation purposes during the dry season. This spot now provided water for the soul rather than water for the earth. Mehul did not have time to go inside that day but said a brief prayer as he passed by and instantly had the overwhelming feeling that God had something special in store for him.

Not much further down the road in front of a small orphanage, he saw a young woman highlighted by a blinding stream of light that encompassed her whole being. The source seemed to shine from within her as well. The girl looked like an angel sent from heaven. Usually a shy man, Mehul felt prompted to stop and watch the girl. She was not like anyone he had ever seen.

The woman of light worked with the abandoned children in a gentle manner and appeared to be teaching them to read. Mehul did not know how to read himself. He imagined how wonderful it would be to have this woman teach his children how to read one day. Then he imagined how incredible it would be to have this woman as more than a teacher of his children, but their own mother. Mehul knew that it would never be possible and shook the thought from his head, but it would not go away. He watched her for so long that he almost forgot the errand he had been sent on, but eventually completed his task and then looked for the brilliant girl again on his way back by. The children were gone, but she was still outside beside the building hanging out to dry wash that would fit small bodies. She knew how to work too. Even before ever having the courage to speak with her Mehul knew this girl was the gift God had promised him in front of the Sikh temple.

After several visits over many months, Mehul finally convinced the angelic creature to marry him. He had given up the family of his youth to create the family of his adulthood. His mother's brother bequeathed to him a small plot of land since both of his cousins had died leaving it empty. He was still a Sharma, his father had not taken back the name with his disavowal, but that was all he had left from his parents. Mehul

44

prayed he could give his own beta more than his name one day. He tried not to dwell on his other son and daughters who had only received an inheritance of land the size of their small bodies.

Most in India cremated their dead and often scattered the ashes in a sacred body of water, any water was sacred these days, but exceptions were sometimes made for young children and devout older believers. His Hiya could not bear to have the small bodies burned and wanted to keep them near. Mehul believed in reincarnation and that the soul itself was not subject to death, so it had not mattered to him where the bodies were. He knew his children lived on. He tried each day to be sufficiently prayerful with righteous living, so he could break the cycle of birth and death and return to God when his life was over. His children had been pure, perhaps they were already waiting for him there.

He and Hiya were both believers and rarely did their religious views clash. They were able to bury their children in a manner that honored and gave as much peace as possible to them both. Then they carried on, without losing or burying their belief with their losses. Mehul still followed the ritual of Kesh allowing his hair to grow naturally out of respect for the perfection in God's creations. Briary supported him in that practice, she respected the turban that protected his uncut hair and kept it clean. She still read from her book of God's words daily. They loved each other and they loved their God. Sikhs accepted that there were many divine messengers, including Krishna, Moses, Mohammed and even his wife's Jesus. So, while their beliefs may be housed in different buildings, he and his Hiya both worshiped a God who lived in the heavens and looked over them all. A loving God, a forgiving God, and hopefully one that would send rain soon.

Mehul's heart burst with tenderness as he looked back at his young son gathering the scythed jowar plants with his slender sinewy arms and putting them in little piles. The boy looked more like his bride Briary, but he caught glimpses of himself in their son as well. Anoop was a living combination of their love. Their only surviving child. Mehul wondered if God would bless them with more… if either of them could bear the risk.

The swinging sharp blade paused for a moment and Anoop interjected. "Baba can you tell me a story while we work. Your stories always make the time go faster." His eyes pleaded.

"If you can keep up with your gathering and not stop to listen," Mehul answered sternly and then softened. "Do you want to hear a fairytale, a family story or one about India's history?"

"Any of those, baba. You choose." Anoop answered with excitement. He just looked happy to have a diversion.

Mehul did not want to add extra burden to either of them at the moment by talking about tragic family memories and fairytales were for playful times, he would share a moment in history with Anoop. Mehul began sharing the first event that came into his mind.

"Anoop do you remember seeing the large white palace on the south bank of the Yamuna river in Agra?" Mehul asked.

"Yes baba, everyone knows the Taj Mahal." Anoop replied.

"I will tell you how that building came to be. It is not a palace, but a tomb." Mehul began.

"You mean like the graves for our family?" Anoop asked questioningly.

"Yes, but much more magnificent and built by an emperor for his wife." Mehul continued, "Over two hundred years ago the Mughal emperor, Shah Jahan, reigned over India. His third wife, Mumtaz Mahal was his favorite wife and he loved her very much."

"Like you love ma?" Anoop interjected.

Mehul confirmed, "Yes, like I love your ma. Muntaz Mahal was a Persian princess and she died giving birth to their fourteenth child named Gauhara Begum."

"Ma has not had fourteen children. I would be so sad if she died." Anoop shared as he continued gathering.

"I would be so sad if ma died too and Shah Jahan was very very sad. He wanted to honor the memory of his beloved bride, so he asked the court architect to build the most beautiful mausoleum of white marble to bury his wife's body inside. The building took over ten years with over twenty-thousand workers. Then another five years to create the beautiful gardens, a guest house and a stone wall all around it, but when it was finally completed the whole world was inspired by its beauty."

"Did it make Shah Jahan feel better?" Anoop sincerely asked.

"That is a good question Anoop. I am not sure that it did. Because after the Taj Mahal was completed, Shah Jahan wanted to build another one out of black marble across the river from it," Mehul added.

"Did he build it?" Anoop asked. "How come I have never seen it?"

"The black Taj Mahal was never built. Shah Jahan's son Aurangzeb was upset that his father was spending all of his inheritance on these extravagant buildings and imprisoned the emperor under house arrest. Shah Jahan was only able to view the Taj Mahal from his window for the last eight years of his life before being entombed there with his beloved wife after he died."

"I would never put you in a prison baba, even if you did spend all of my money," Anoop assured.

"I am sure you wouldn't beta." Mehul chuckled. "Do not fear, there would not be much to spend anyway, we who earn only a few rupees a year cannot even imagine that many rupees in our whole lifetime."

The story had made the work go faster and Mehul was able to give his son a history lesson as they toiled. Mehul was blessed with a very good boy who would never put Mehul in prison and could hopefully help him harvest enough food to fill their bellies over the cold season. Those blessings were good and enough.

Chapter 5 notes: The Taj Mahal is sometimes called a "teardrop on the cheek of time". The story Mehul told Anoop is based on the recorded history behind its construction. It is considered one of the seven wonders of the world and the original cost to build was estimated at 32 million rupees. In 2015 that cost would be approximately 52.8 billion rupees or $827 million in U.S. currency. The information about the **Gurudwara Guru Ka Taal** temple in Agra is also based on fact.

Chapter 6 – NYC 2020

Blaze

"I am either
a storm
or
a drought.
In-betweens
have never
been my thing."
- Sanober Kha

Wall Street was all abuzz on a Monday morning. How could anyone not love the energy of Manhattan? International finance made Blaze's blood pump faster and gave purpose to his life. Brooke was missing out on all the adventures of the city by living way out in the wild west. A person could not even get a decent cannoli in Oregon. Blaze downed the Italian pastry with a quick cup of coffee and headed to the office.

Kylie greeted him with a list of pending mergers and calls to return as he walked through the door. The girl was a

50

stunner with her tall, toned body that gave off an air of allure even in boxy fitted suits. Long dark hair was pulled back from her face and intelligent eyes gave him no indication of any interest beyond business. That was one of the reasons he had hired her in the first place. Kylie's moral code of ethics, which made her a trustworthy assistant, also translated into her personal life and kept her out of his bedroom. With a wife three-thousand miles away it would have been convenient to have an assistant that did double duty, but Blaze had given Kylie enough opportunities. He knew the enhanced relationship was not going to happen and he was careful not to risk a sexual harassment suit. The girl was too good at what she did in the office to lose her on a dalliance.

"Anson Bailey called and would like a return call as soon as possible. Then the Carson-Peck merger meeting is on the docket for eleven." Kylie reminded her boss.

"Yes Kylie, I did have a stimulating weekend, so glad you asked." Blaze coolly interjected as he looked over the day's schedule that she handed him.

"Sorry Mr. Ridgeway, I have today on the brain. Did your weekend go well?" Kylie added.

"How many times do I need to remind you to call me Blaze. You make me feel like I am old enough to be your father when you call me by my father's name. And yes, I did some rowing on the Hudson yesterday at the Yonkers Club. Quite invigorating." Blaze knew that he actually was old enough to be her father, but he did not like to be reminded of the fact. He was a fit fifty-two who could pass for five to ten years younger and usually did. He swallowed the inclination to ask her to join him on the water next time and instead went into his office to begin his day. Why waste energy on actions with no return value. There were plenty of women who would be interested, but none that he could take as an escort to any of the social events and functions that he was expected to attend.

It would have been so much easier if Brooke had stayed in NYC. Blaze would never have imagined that an actress would have had such strong mothering instincts. Their children were not planned. Blaze didn't like anything unplanned and he had never really wanted children to begin with. Maybe one healthy son to pass on his financial fortune and DNA would have been okay. But Blaze did not get a *normal* son and an additional unexpected daughter came along in the package deal. Then there was the fact that his wife took better care of the twins than she did of him. Things had gone horribly wrong. If he tried to get out of the marriage at this point, he would look like the bad guy and that would never do. Blaze had an impeccable image to maintain. He had groomed his reputation for years. A man who abandoned a wife and his two children, one of the two who happened to be handicapped, might not be seen as reliable in his business dealings either.

Blaze buzzed Kylie on the intercom. "Kylie, could you research live-in facilities or group homes for special needs adults, who are eighteen years old or older?'

"Sure, Mr. Ridgeway, I mean Blaze. Could you give me any more details on what you would like me to look for?" Kylie tried to clarify. "What business file will it be under?"

"Not business, personal... just look up any highly rated, long-term institutions that are available. Make a list of the location, price, any necessary qualifications of the candidates." Blaze instructed.

"I am on it." Kylie, not one to chatter, signed off.

Blaze had the preliminary idea of a fantastic plan come into his mind. His twins were nearly sixteen. In a few more years his daughter would be off to college leaving only the boy at home. Blaze doubted his autistic son would be able to go to college, but at eighteen he would be legally an adult. He should not need a mommy to hold his hand anymore. If Blaze could find an appropriate adult group home for him, Brooke could come back to New York. Things could go back to how they were before the diapered duo crossed their doorstep.

An incoming text vibrated his phone. Blaze opened the message to view the photo of a mangy looking pup with words of explanation typed beneath, "Maybe this little guy could keep you company in NY dad…so you don't get lonely," followed by a heart emoji. It was from Juniper.

It appeared daughters were not all bad. His daughter seemed to have a soft heart and she imagined that somehow, he did too. Maybe he should invite the girl to the Big Apple some time to experience life in the city. She seemed sharp enough to appreciate it. He, or Kylie, could share a few of New York's best museums with her, take in a stroll through Central Park, or even escort the girl on an evening date to the theater in Brooke's honor. His daughter might even return to Oregon an emissary of goodwill to help convince her hesitant mother to return. However, the dog Juniper was suggesting that he give sanctuary to via this text was about the last warm body he wanted taking up space in his brownstone.

Chapter 7 – Oregon 2020

Conifer

"God has cared for these trees, saved them from drought, disease, avalanches, and a thousand tempests and floods. But he cannot save them from fools." - *John Muir*

Conifer clutched his book of trees like it was a precious Bible. Trees were his favorite plant in the world of botany. The book listed varieties of trees by their genus, location of growth and characteristics. Trees were his living, breathing friends. They provided the oxygen that helped keep him and others alive. He didn't need to worry about losing them. They didn't run away, and trees tended to be long-lived perennial plants, some reaching several thousand years old. It was estimated that there were just over three-trillion mature trees in the world today composed of over sixty-thousand species. That fact alone blew his already cluttered mind. There were two main types of trees: deciduous and evergreen. Deciduous trees lost all of their leaves for part of the year. In cold climates, this happened during the autumn so that the trees were bare throughout the winter. In hot and dry climates, deciduous trees usually lost their leaves during the dry season. Their loss of leaves gave Conifer a feeling of nakedness, fully clothed evergreen trees were his favorites. They fascinated him. He and his sister were evergreens.

Juniper leaves could either be like needles or scales; most of the species changed from needle form to scale form as they matured. His Juniper was not prickly even now, but it would be interesting to watch how she developed. Her tree grew fast to fifteen feet. His sister Juniper was not that tall, but definitely taller for a girl than he was for a boy. And most junipers were created with at least some level of drought resistance. His sister was definitely more resilient than he was in many ways.

Although the total number of species of conifers was relatively small (making him the rarer variety), conifers were considered ecologically important. His namesake was not worthless. Conifers were the dominant plants over the taiga of the Northern Hemisphere, but also in similar cool climates in mountains further south. Boreal conifers made wintertime adaptations, so his tree was at least adaptable even if he wasn't so much. The narrow conical shape of northern conifers, and their downward-drooping limbs, helped them shed snow. He hoped he could learn to sluff off things that made him freeze up too. The book said many conifers seasonally altered their biochemistry to make them more resistant to freezing.

Conifer closed the book. He did not need it open to know what it said. He had memorized most of the pages and knew them by heart. The plant world made sense. It gave him comfort and a peaceful place to exist. He did not have to interpret their facial expressions, their tone of voice or their many moods. Maybe their body language could be interpreted some, a drooping plant usually needed more water. They were living creatures that did not complicate his life. His new school focused more on interacting with plants than stressful social situations and he flourished in that safer soil.

As an extra credit project Conifer had created his own garden in their backyard which would continue to grow over the summer. There was no room to plant a forest back there, but he had lined the fence of the yard with thirty species of deciduous and evergreen trees alternately. Then he had plowed a twenty by thirty-foot area of the rich, loamy volcanic soil and created long parallel furrows to hold the water needed to give life to the seeds he planted in each elevated row. Green shoots of carrots, lettuce, corn, and peas were just poking their heads out of the earth. He had planted the corn that would eventually grow quite tall in the back row and he would need to add stakes soon for the pea plants to climb. The tomato plants he had started in the house over a month ago and then added them to their rows outside already partially grown so that the fruit would have time to mature before the growing season ended. To the south side of the garden plot, he made mounds of dirt to plant cucumber, squash and pumpkin seeds in. He felt like a full-on farmer and nurturer of Mother Nature's bounty. The garden was his happy place.

His mother left him alone on the sofa and was talking to his sister about getting her driving permit. He could tell that his sister and mother worked hard to be a part of his life and that they cared about him very much, but it was frustrating that he was never able to give them what they needed from him in return. His father caused him the most stress. Not only could Conifer never give the man what he wanted, but his dad also scared him for some reason too. Things were much better here, out of the way in Oregon.

The easiest human to talk to in Conifer's world was a person that he couldn't even see. Maybe that helped take away the pressure. Conifer didn't have to deal with facial expressions or voice intonations either. His friend spoke straight into his head. Conifer did not hear the words with his ears, but with his mind. Their communication was not as confusing or jumbly as the rest. It was calm and direct, like a ray of light creating photosynthesis on a green leaf. He could process this communication without peripheral interruptions. Conifer did not have to draw upon premade song sentences from his mental library like those he used with other people; he could send his thought waves directly back to this friend to interpret.

The person had not yet shared his name and Conifer had not thought to ask but merely referred to him (he assumed it was a him) as *Neem* after a large tree with bright leaves that fulfilled many purposes for good. Tree names made sense in his world. The neem tree's wood was used to make furniture and its leaves and bark to make medicines for various diseases and disorders. Yes, whatever his real name happened to be; Neem was a healing influence in Conifer's life. When his thoughts got tangled Neem helped him make sense of what was going on around him and Neem supported Conifer's research into the plant world. Neem seemed to love growing things as much as Conifer did. But it was impossible to help his mother and Juniper understand that he was not alone, that he had a friend, the best of friends right beside him or within him almost every day.

Conifer headed out back to check on his garden. When he was outside in nature his mind worked the best. For some reason, he didn't get over-stimulated the way he did indoors.

He knew there was just as much, if not more, input going on around him, but it was different, cleaner, clearer. Neem joined him as Conifer turned on the hose to begin watering. The non-verbal voice welcomed him with a gentle comment on how well the corn was doing. Conifer responded mentally in agreement. Then the topic turned a corner Conifer had not rounded yet.

"Conifer, you have been blessed with a gift. You could use your skills with plants for good in this world," Neem complimented. "Have you considered studying horticulture or agriculture in college? Or you could even become an arborist since you love trees so much. Dendrology is the study of wooded plants."

Conifer had not thought that far ahead. He liked to study and got good grades in school, but he unusually took one day at a time thinking about what was right in front of him. "I am not sure what I am going to do after high school, but I do love working with things that grow. I am not sure if I could get into a college program."

"Of course, you could," Neem encouraged. "You will just need to make sure you prepare yourself to be able to get accepted into a university, one that can help you develop your unique talents."

"What will I need to do?" Conifer asked his friend.

"You are already doing the usual college prep stuff, like studying and getting good grades. You will need to take some entrance exams like the SAT or ACT, but there may be more we can do to get you on the radar of a college with a high-level science department. Maybe we can come up with a great science fair project for you for next year."

Conifer loved science fairs but had never participated before. The thought of giving a presentation seemed above and beyond him. As this fear formed in his mind Neem was ready with a reply.

"You can present most of your data in poster form that people can read for themselves. Then you will only need a few memorized statements to share, maybe Juniper can even help you with the verbal parts if it is allowed and you know I would be there to assist as well." Neem offered. "It is something to think about anyway."

"If I can come up with a viable project maybe I will give it a try," Conifer replied cautiously in his thoughts. He did not want to commit yet to something that might be out of his scope. "Thank you for your support," he added. "I think I would like to go to college if one would take me."

Conifer was lucky to have Neem share with him ideas that he may not think of on his own. Neem made him stretch and grow. His mother was helpful but too protective and she did not push him out of his comfort zone. As that thought crossed his mind, his mother came through the back door and joined him beside his garden.

"Looks like everything is coming up nicely Conifer. We are going to have some delicious fresh vegetables to add to our dinners soon - healthy as well as tasty." She smiled.

Conifer tried to imitate her smile and reflect it back to her but was not sure he got it right. His smiles usually looked like he was in pain instead of happy when he practiced them in the mirror.

"Is there anything you would like for dinner tonight?" His mother asked.

Unfortunately, his mother could not read his mind like Neem could, but she was patient and willing to wait for a verbal response from him. The first semi-appropriate answer that came out of his mouth was a Jack Johnson lyric, "…*Make you banana pancakes. Pretend like it's the weekend now.*" Conifer did like pancakes for dinner.

"Breakfast for dinner it is." His mom supported his suggestion cheerfully. She made his efforts easy by being thrilled with pretty much anything he said. Hopefully Juniper would like to eat pancakes tonight too.

Chapter 7 notes: The neem tree leaf is used for leprosy, eye disorders, bloody noses, intestinal worms, upset stomachs, loss of appetite, skin ulcers, diseases of the heart and blood vessels (cardio-vascular disease), fevers, diabetes, gum disease (gingivitis), and liver problems. The leaf is also used for birth control.

Autism spectrum disorder is a developmental disability that generally appears before the age of 3 and now affects 1 in 68 children. Boys are nearly 5 times more likely than girls to be diagnosed with ASD. Autism spectrum disorder is one of the fastest-growing developmental disorders in the United States. ASD is more common than childhood cancer, diabetes and AIDS combined. The term stems from the Greek word autos meaning "self", autism literally means "alone".

Conifer's song lyrics- *Banana Pancakes* by Jack Johnson

Chapter 8 – India 1877

Anoop

(Hindi: अनूप) is a masculine given name. The Sanskrit word *anūpa* has the following meanings: *watery, situated near the water, bank of a river, pond, lagoon.*
The meaning of the name *Anoop* is:
Incomparable, unequaled; unique; pond.

"We have been living through a time of sorrow. Our seed remains seed. Our nostrils are dusty."
-Warren Eyster, The Goblins of Eros

The Sharma family was down to only one meal a day. Anoop's parents chose to eat the midday meal and gave Anoop more than his share even when he protested. Something was better than nothing. His family was surviving the dry spell better than some of their neighbors, because his baba had carefully rationed last year's sparse harvest.

The rains had not come to enable any kind of crop to grow for the new season. Their seeds lay asleep in the earth not getting their morning drink still covered by a dry dirt blanket. Anoop could not imagine what this harvest would bring…it looked like nothing. Dust puffed into the air with every footstep as he walked across their parched land. He would likely be lying next to his siblings before another year passed if things did not improve. Anoop's given name meant *watery pond* and his middle name was his mother's surname, Fountain. He was literally a water fountain. It was too bad he could not magically spout the much-needed water to wet their land. Baba said this was the worst drought his country had seen for one-hundred years. Millions had died during the last one. They needed water.

In the distance Anoop saw a horse with rider. It must be an imaginary vision created by his hunger since no one had horses around Agra these days. Most horses had dropped dead from thirst or been eaten. As the appearing-to-be-real horse drew closer, it looked as if its destination was actually the Sharma home. The unknown rider on a white horse with brown patches pulled to a stop in front of their mud block hut with a thatched roof. Ma rushed from the house and impulsively threw her arms around the elderly Englishman who had dropped down from the overheated animal's back.

"Anoop, say hello to your Grandfather Tristan." Ma instructed as she backed away suddenly becoming reserved again.

It had been so long since his dada had visited that Anoop did not remember his face. The man's skin and eyes were lighter colored like Ma's, and he could see some of her features reflected in the grandpa before him. Anoop had never ever seen his dadi and nani on his baba's side, that he was aware of anyway, so having a grandparent here was a real treat. Even if Anoop knew his ma would worry about what to feed the extra mouth. These thoughts crossed Anoop's mind as he bowed with respect and said, "Namaste Dada Tristan."

The man extended his large hand for Anoop to shake and replied, "Nice to officially meet my grandson." Anoop took the hand and hesitated to let go. He wanted his dada to stay.

'What brings you here, father?" Ma asked.

"Can't a man check in on his family Briary?" Grandpa Tristan answered. "I know food has been scarce in this area, so I brought some supplies to help tide you over this tough time."

"It is interesting that the English continue to eat well, while many in India starve." Ma spoke almost angrily to her father which was not at all like the ma that Anoop knew. "Why

66

does Great Britain continue to export our crops when we need all that we have grown to stay here to feed the people?"

"Briary, I am here now sharing food with you. Not all food is sent out of the country. Please, can I come in and sit for a bit and get to know my grandson? Take the food if only for him." His dada requested.

Anoop was afraid his mother would send her father and the food away in her anger and he was not ready for his grandfather to go. Anoop went up to the canvas sacks slung over the horse's back and placed his hand on the bulging bag wondering what was inside. His mother needed to keep whatever the bag held. Perhaps they could even share some with their neighbors. The Khatri family had already lost a child due to hunger.

"Mehul would not like us taking charity from you, he is away looking for work in town, but I am truly grateful. Do come in, but know I have little to offer you." Ma looked sad and happy at the same time.

No rain had fallen in many months, the rivers nearby had gone dry, but ma was still able to draw some drinking water from their shallow well and offer her father a drink. They were blessed that the well had not dried up yet. For family members who had not seen one another in such a long time, Anoop did not think the two had much to say to one another. Anoop wanted to ask all about other family members, ones that he had never met, and what it was like working for the British East India Company. But instead, he respectfully listened to his mother and grandfather politely converse about the problematic weather pattern before watching dada Tristan ride away on his horse. His grandfather must have gotten to know him quickly. Anoop was not ready to have the man go.

"I will do something great like dada one day. I will have a good job and be able to bring food to my family too," Anoop thought. His grandpa Tristan was the closest thing to a hero Anoop had ever met. Maybe not really a real hero, but the man was bigger than life and he could ride off into the sunset on a horse. That seemed magical through his young eyes.

Baba Mehul came home before dark to find food in the house and dinner on the table that Grandpa Tristan had provided but had refused to stay and share.

"He was here?" his father said flatly knowing where the food came from without being told.

"Yes Mehul, please do not be angry." His ma replied.

"How can I be angry with him when I cannot feed my family? Do you think my pride would let you and Anoop starve?" Baba said sadly. "I only wish we could share some of the food with my brother's families. Maybe my uncle can let them know we have some to share."

Anoop ate his portion of rice and cabbage with gusto. Then asked to be excused. He rushed out the door to go visit his siblings and let them know their dada had visited and brought the family food. His siblings had not gotten to spend time with their grandfather or received any gifts, so Anoop needed to make sure he shared the experience with them. There were no jowar leaves surrounding the graves anymore and the sun had baked the mounds hard packed making them not as comfortable to lie or sit between, but it was still Anoop's favorite place to be on the farm.

A full moon added light to the darkening sky as Anoop searched for inspiration. What could he do in the name of the six Sharma children? How could he bring honor and blessings to his family in their names? He would love to be able to provide food, but that required bringing water. He doubted he could direct to or create water on their land. He was not a rainmaker. Should he go into the city to find work or was he needed more here? The burden of being the one living was unexpected. How could life over death be harder? But what could one young boy do to make a difference? He would find the answer. His sisters and brother would help him figure it out.

His big brother Reyansh would be twelve years now. He would be a bigger help to their baba if he were here, but even Reyansh could not bring the rain. Anoop remembered catching tree frogs with Reyansh down by the stream - its bed now dry. The frogs' yellowish-green slimy bodies would slip out of Anoop's small hands, but Reyansh could cup his hands around them and hold the little fellows inside. Once in a while a webbed foot would poke its way through his brother's fingers, or a muffled croaking sound could be heard coming from between his brother's palms. Reyansh never hurt the frogs, but they were a challenge to catch and fun to scare their sisters with on occasion. Anoop wondered if the frogs were gone now too.

The words to *Amazing Grace* in his mother's clear soprano voice filled the night sky… "*amazing grace, how sweet the sound that saved a wretch like me, I once was lost, but now am found, t'was blind but now I see*"… Anoop was not blind, but maybe wretched and he could use some saving, the whole family could. He needed to find some of this *grace* his ma liked to sing about. Then maybe he could do something wonderful and important. Anoop patted the earthen mound where his brother lay. There would always be a connection between them.

"Reyansh, my brother, if it is possible could you please send some water or maybe some grace our way... from wherever you are? That would be wonderful. Thanks, this is Anoop."

Anoop knew Reyansh was not a god, but he also knew that his brother would be the first one to help his family if there was any way he was able to. The round moon's light bathed the area with a holy softness full of hope. Filled with peace and a full belly for the first time in days, Anoop rolled over and went to sleep right where he was.

Chapter 11 notes: Great Britain continued to heavily export crops from India throughout the famine and also greatly reduced welfare spending towards India and other territories during that time.

The author of the hymn *Amazing Grace* was, by his own admission, a "wretch." John Newton was a slave trader, a blasphemer, a rebel, an immoral man, a torturer, and as far from grace as anyone could ever be. When he was eleven, young John launched into that exciting life of voyaging, sailing, and living his dream. But the dream turned out to be a nightmare. Later in life he wrote, "I sinned with a high hand, and I made it my study to tempt and seduce others." Newton lived a hard life with hard consequences. God got his attention though. In 1748, Newton's slave ship was nearly wrecked by an intense storm. In the tempest, surrounded by crashing waves, cutting winds, creaking timbers, and the cries of onboard slaves, John fell to his knees and pled for mercy, and for grace. God's grace, which reaches anyone, anywhere, saved a wretch like John Newton. Newton wrote the song years later while serving as a pastor in Olney, England.

Chapter 9 – Oregon 2020

Juniper

"There is a lot that happens around the world that we cannot control. We cannot stop earthquakes, we cannot prevent droughts, and we cannot prevent all conflict, but when we know where the hungry, the homeless, and the sick exist, then we can help."- Jan Schakowasky

All of the furry Avengers had been placed at what would hopefully become good homes, besides Juniper's favorite buddy Dr. Strange. Juniper had written each of the pup's names that she bequeathed them with on their adoption application papers before sending them off, but was pretty sure they would be renamed immediately by their new owners. She wondered what prospective adoptees found wrong with this little guy who had been left behind. Dr. Strange cocked his head with one blue and one brown eye looking up expectantly at her. Those begging eyes were even a mixture of her and her brother. How could she leave him here without the rest of his team? There is no way she would have considered taking him home if he didn't seem so lonely without his siblings.

Juniper sat on the less-than-spotless kennel floor with the solo remaining puppy and filled out her own paperwork to adopt the dog. It was unlikely her mother would agree to the acquisition, but Brooke did have a soft heart, Juniper could play to that. Juniper decided if she could get the canine through the door and hide him for a few days - or weeks if needed - her mother would hopefully not have the heart to send back the newest family member. Brooke was all about not rejecting those that needed extra love. Her father, on the other hand, might be another story. His response to her text about considering Dr. Strange as a roommate in NYC had been less than encouraging. It included the suggestion to sell the freak dog to the circus. Were there even circuses around anymore? Her dad must have watched *The Greatest Showman* recently. Dr. Strange was not a freak, more like unique. He would fit in just fine at their house either way.

The sandpapery tongue licked Juniper's hand. Dr. Strange was already saying thank you. This pup's good manners would help with the homebound relocation plan, but Juniper wasn't ready to take Dr. Strange home today. She needed to make a few undercover preparations at home first. A couple more days in the kennel should be okay.

"Do you really plan to take that pup home with you Juni-per? I thought your mom wouldn't approve." Arriving as silent as a ninja, Stetson asked Juniper while reading the paperwork over her shoulder. He always pronounced her name with a tiny break in it that made it almost sound like two separate words.

"I could tell you that my mom changed her mind, but that comment may be a bit premature. Let's just say it is a work in progress," Juniper admitted. "I feel a special connection with this pup and can't leave him here all alone. I have a positive feeling about it working out."

"You have a special connection with all of the dogs here Juni-per Ridgeway. That's why you make such a great volunteer. You will end up with a dozen dogs on your doorstep if you're not careful. You're going to have to develop some objectivity." Stetson shared gently.

"I know, I know. But just one will be okay," Juniper said more to herself than to Stetson.

"Hey, did you get your driving permit yet." Stetson smoothly changed the subject.

"As a matter of fact, I did. Not sure when I will get to practice, but I have taken the first step to becoming an official Oregon driver." Juniper proudly replied.

"How about I give you your first lesson? I'm a patient instructor and maybe my dad will even lend us his old-school stick shift. It is a little trickier but would make you mega prepared." Stetson offered.

The thought of another option besides her intense and over-booked mother giving her tips behind the wheel sounded blissful to Juniper. "If you think you can handle it, I am down for a lesson from the Stetson Buttars school of driving instruction," Juniper joked.

"How about I drop by Saturday morning around ten?" Stetson asked looking at her directly, intense violet eyes peeking through his black bangs.

How did a girl say no to that? "Sounds great unless my mom has different plans for me," Juniper mentally scheduled.

"It's a date then." Stetson answered as he ambled away.

Wait, did he mean a date-date? Or was that just something guys said, like it was now a date on their calendar? Juniper had no reason to think Stetson would want anything near an actual date with her and driving practice was not what anyone would call romantic. Don't read anything into his simple offer Juniper told herself. But the thought did make her feel nervous and slightly giddy.

No one was home when Juniper arrived. Conifer must have had an appointment that she had forgotten about. So, she had time to check out temporary holding quarters for her wannabe pet. Dr. Strange was not a yippy dog, he just needed some private space for a few days for everyone to get used to the idea - mostly her mother. Conifer shouldn't have a problem; her brother would be mostly oblivious to another living being in their house she supposed. Juniper emptied her laundry basket onto her bedroom floor, grabbed her super-soft, pre-school blankie from her dresser drawer to line the bottom and tossed in her favorite stuffed monkey then tucked the makeshift puppy layette under her bed to wait for its impending tenant. If hiding him here didn't work, she would smuggle Dr. Strange to school. Now all she needed was puppy food and a water bowl.

The rest of her family still wasn't around when she finished, so Juniper grabbed a snack and turned on the computer. There was always homework to be done, but Juniper wasn't in the mood. She had recently discovered an online site called Ancestry.com and had begun to dabble in searching through it. Her mother never talked much about their family background and it was like her father dropped onto earth from another planet. There was nothing she could find out about him and her father's ancestors were non-existent. Had the man changed his name or identity at some point she wondered? She tried not to be skeptical about her absentee dad.

Juniper had been able to research back a few hundred years in her mother's family history. She watched a YouTube video to figure out how to jump the ocean or *cross the pond* as her British ancestors would say. No one was a natural-born or a native American much before the 1800s, except the actual native American Indians. Brooke's maiden name Fountain hailed from England and it looked like most of them were still living there. Juniper could get lost digging through her ancestors for hours, but her mom and brother would be home before too long and it would be nice if she started something for dinner. Maybe Juniper could earn some goodwill points for her dog request as well as her driving "date" on Saturday.

Hot angel hair pasta with marinara sauce and a fresh green salad were ready when she heard their car pull into the driveway. Her mom's cheerful smile and "smells delicious" comment as she walked through the front door gave Juniper a glimmer of hope that the dinner might actually move her dog-convincing mission a few steps forward.

Saturday morning Stetson showed up for her driving lesson in a bomber jacket and aviator sunglasses. He looked official or at least officially handsome for the adventure.

"Are you ready to get some hours behind the wheel, my favorite dog volunteer?" Stetson asked as she opened the front door.

After the spaghetti dinner her mother had agreed to let her go driving today. Then this morning at the last minute, she suggested maybe Juniper could take Conifer along "for the experience". More likely for a chaperone Juniper guessed. She did not think her brother would have any interest in joining their "date" as a back-seat driver, but he had perked up at the idea. *Get outta my dreams and into my car*," was Conifer's actual vocal response.

"I am so ready, but would you mind a tagalong?" Juniper awkwardly asked. "My mom thought it might be nice for Conifer to join us. Not to drive, but to watch and socialize." How embarrassing, Juniper would never have asked, but she was still gathering goodwill puppy points.

Stetson did not miss a beat, "I have wanted to meet your brother, sure bring him along."

Stetson said he decided not to start her on the stick shift car, so had brought his old beater to practice for the first time. Conifer, not as stiff as usual, followed them out to the 2002 Chevy Impala.

"Ready for a ride buddy?" Stetson asked Conifer as he put out his hand to shake Conifers.

Conifer replied without hesitation, *"Life is a highway I want to ride it all night long. If you're going my way, I want to drive it all night long."* He nearly looked Stetson in the eyes as he accepted his hand in a fish-like wimpy shake. This was going to be an interesting ride and not probably the "date" that Stetson had imagined, but he was being an extremely good sport about the whole thing and didn't even have to stifle a laugh at Conifer's "drive all night long" comment.

Juniper watched from the passenger's seat and Conifer from the back as Stetson went over basic rules of driving while he drove across town to an old abandoned speedway. Her resourceful dog rescue friend had somehow gotten permission for them to use the track for a beginner driver to practice on…or perhaps they were trespassing. Either way, it was an incredible spot.

"I know there is not much distance in the straight-away patches of pavement but driving straight is easy. I thought we could practice starts, stops, curves and if you feel ready parking." Stetson suggested.

He traded places with Juniper, and she adjusted the mirrors as he had shown. Then she put her hands in the ten-o'clock-two-o'clock position on the steering wheel before giving the gas pedal a little push. Well maybe more than a little push, the car lurched to a very fast start for an old vehicle. She hit the first turn going far too fast and Stetson had to reach over and grab the steering wheel to help make a sharp enough turn to prevent an off-roading experience. They coasted to a stop and Juniper's heart was racing. It could have been because she was scared, but it was the first time a boy had ever touched her - besides her brother who didn't count and didn't even like to be touched. Stetson's hand on top of hers had sent chills up her whole arm and all of its little hairs were standing on end.

"Whoa girl, you don't need to be Mario Andretti." Stetson teased. "Let's ease up on that lead foot even though we are on a racetrack."

Juniper was not sure who Mario Andretti was, but she assumed he drove too fast. Conifer seemed unusually calm for a near-death experience - or at least a less than controlled ride. Stetson was ready to go again right away and wanted to make sure she "got right back on the horse". They did about twenty loops with starts and stops and Juniper got better each time around. She was actually getting the hang of it. Once Juniper seemed semi-comfortable with her driving, Stetson broadened the topic of conversation.

"I noticed your Dr. dog is still in the kennel at the rescue, did you change your mind?"

"No, just waiting for the perfect timing. I think maybe Monday, but..." Juniper nodded her head towards the back seat, "doesn't know."

Stetson picked up on the not so subtle head motions and turned to Conifer to cover his blooper, "hey back seat driver would you like a turn behind the wheel."

Conifer who paid very close attention to details, first response was a questioning, "Snoop Dog?" He had definitely not missed the dog question. Then he followed with an answer to the driving question, *"On the road again, I just can't wait to get on the road again. Goin' places that I've never been..."* He was already climbing out of the back seat to give driving a try.

Juniper knew her mother would not be thrilled, but Conifer sure looked like he was as he rounded the first turn of the racetrack. He was not the best driver, but not worse than she was her first time around. Conifer stopped and started every few feet jerking as he hit the gas and brake pads intermittently, but at least he made the corner turn without assistance. He even monotone rapped out some more of Willie

Nelson's song as they started their second loop. *"Here we go, on the road again, like a band of gypsies we go down the highway. We're the best of friends…"*

Stetson laughed. The guy was pretty cool. He didn't make fun of her brother and seemed to get him. Juniper worked hard to keep tears from welling up in her eyes. This had been the best "date" she had ever had. It didn't matter that it was her first and only date. She was not sure if any in the future could top it. She joined in on Stetson's chuckles; this was the first time that laughing at her brother felt okay.

Chapter 9 notes: Song lyrics Conifer spoke - *Get Outta My Dreams and into My Car* by Billy Ocean. *Life is a Highway* by Tom Cochran. *On the Road Again* by Willie Nelson.

Chapter 10 – Oregon 2020

Brooke/Blaze

*"My grandmother used to say God gives us drought years-
years drained of happiness- to prepare for bounteous times.
I am more than ready for the bounty"-Ellen Hopkins*

Blaze's more or less quarterly check-in visit was
scheduled to begin today. Brooke knew she should be more
excited. She loved her husband, at least she thought she did,
but she was not sure how much she liked him. Let's just say
her life was easier when he was away. She had planned to pick
Blaze up at the airport, but when she mentioned to him that he
would need to drive her to her Autism Awareness meeting and
to her Oak Leaf Academy volunteer assignment since they
only had one car here, he had opted to rent his own vehicle.
That would be easier for both of them.

Brooke tidied up their bedroom - it was really more
just hers - for guest husband. She almost wished they had twin
beds in the room like in the old 1950s sitcoms. It wasn't that

she was averse to touch like her son. Brooke had been living like a nun for the past few months and could use some intimacy, but for some reason being with Blaze almost made her feel violated. What a horrible wife she was. She should be more grateful for the way of life he provided for them and for being able to live where it was best for Conifer. Brooke knew her absence was a sacrifice for Blaze. She needed to think more positively about the man.

The kids seemed on edge in anticipation of the visit as well. There was a non-tangible heaviness descending over the whole household. Maybe it was just her imagination. She did let it run away with her at times. Yesterday she thought she heard a dog yipping and she knew they didn't have a dog in their home.

Bigger-than-life Blaze burst through the front door bearing gifts. He did like to make a grand entrance and gifts were one of his love languages. However, the gifts he brought, ones that Kylie had probably purchased for him, were less what the recipients would want and more what Blaze wanted them to have. She reminded herself it was still nice that he made the effort. There was a New York Yankees baseball cap for Conifer, Brooke was not sure how the hat would work with his ever-present headphone attire, maybe beneath? For Juniper there was a cute kitty stuffed animal, not only was

Juniper pretty much past the stuffed animal phase at fifteen, but cats had never been her thing. She was allergic.

Brooke pulled from her gift bag a slinky cocktail dress. She was not sure where she would wear it in Bend, but she thanked Blaze for remembering her so generously.

"I don't want you to start looking like Annie Oakley out here in the wild west. Maybe you can wear the dress for some of your fundraising benefits or keep it to wear in New York when you come home." Blaze informed his wife.

Interestingly Brooke felt more at home here, than she ever had in NYC. It had become clear that Oregon would never be Blaze's home, but she wished there was something in the area he found to enjoy on his visits. She felt pressure trying to keep him happy while he was here. Wasn't wherever your spouse was supposed to feel like home? She could have Conifer show Blaze his garden, but that would be awkward for both of them. Brooke had never looked for, or fell for, another man. There was something powerful and even good somewhere in this guy. She just wished she was better at bringing it out.

"What would you like to do during your time here?" Brooke asked. His stays always went better if Blaze picked how and where to spend his time.

"Just need to spend some time with my beautiful wife and make sure my kids don't forget who I am," Blaze answered almost honestly. This would be a long few days for them all, often with unexpected chaos left behind in Blaze's exiting wake.

If the truth were known Blaze hated coming to Oregon. He wasted a whole day each way flying across the country and there was not much for him to do when he was here. Two days was getting to be the limit he could endure in this rural world. He told himself he was good at checking in on all of his assets and his family was not a liability to him yet. It was not like he couldn't be away from his business, Kylie handled things well when he was gone and much of what he did could be taken care of online anywhere these days. Many businessmen in the city worked remotely and just flew in or took the train to the city for a few days a week, but Blaze could not bear the drudgery of suburbia.

When Blaze arrived on Sunday, he was greeted with a family dinner and then for the most part they just hung around the house. The kids asked him to play games, well Juniper asked, and Conifer endured the experience as well. Monopoly was about the only boardgame Blaze could handle, and that game only lasted one round. There was a brief after-dinner interlude to trek down to Drake Park on the Deschutes River where idyllic families flanked them picnicking and kayaking as the Ridgeways stood and stared at the water until they headed back home. Nature did not relax Blaze. It made him more uptight.

Today was Tuesday and Blaze's flight was scheduled out this evening. He would say goodbye to the kids after school and then head to the airport. Just a few more hours and he was out of this place. Brooke had asked him to pick up Conifer from school since she had a meeting and Juniper would be at the dang dog rescue. The girl took after her mother in being a constant do-gooder.

This morning had been awkward. While Blaze was packing to go, he swore that he heard a dog and went to investigate. Sure enough, in the girl's bedroom he found the furball from the text she sent him peeking out from under her bed.

"What in the world is that doing here, I thought I suggested the circus?" Blaze commented as Juniper returned from the bathroom ready for school.

"Dr. Strange is just here for a school project," Juniper answered as she tucked the little guy into her backpack without zipping it all the way closed so that the animal could get air. "Oh, and I am working on another project for school that maybe you could help me with. Where can I find information on your ancestors? I cannot seem to pull up any on Ancestors.com. It is like they are invisible or non-existent."

The girl was good, deflecting the dog issue by taking the offensive with a question for him. Blaze was not about to get into his background at this point with his daughter, she had won this round. "I am not sure about that ancestor site, perhaps it is not accurate. I will have Kylie send you some information on my family background when I get back to New York." He had prepared a bio with his preferred background information that he sent out to all of his clients.

The father/daughter duo looked into each other's brown eyes. Juniper's were still a milk chocolate brown, but Blaze's had faded to a non-descript bland color. There was something about the girl that he actually did like. She was feisty and had potential. He had read somewhere online that a father's relationship with his daughter(s) was important for healthy development of their self-image, but he had no idea where to begin. The two called an unspoken standoff before Juniper straightened the dog-inhabited backpack on her shoulders, picked up her books and headed out the door to school.

Six hours later Blaze watched as the other twin come out of another school wondering if he was really the father of this one. The autistic boy was a handsome enough lad, but he was so much fairer in coloring than either he or Brooke. And Brooke had worked with some quite attractive men during her theater days. Blaze assumed at the time that most of them did not prefer women partners, so he had no competition. There was an intelligence in the boy's blue eyes when you could get him to look at you. It was just so difficult to communicate with him. Blaze wanted to rip the headphones off the boy's head. Brooke said that they helped Conifer stay calm and not get as anxious by canceling out excessive background noise, but when Conifer was in his car it would be Blaze's rules. No wonder the boy only spoke in song lyrics, that was all he heard.

Blaze realized there was an advantage, he could say what he wanted to the young man here in the car. They could have a father/son heart to heart talk and the boy would not likely hear with those headphones on. Or if he did hear, he probably wouldn't understand what he was hearing. On the longshot that his son did either hear or understand him, who would be able to interpret his song-infested speech pattern even if he tried to share the conversation. This might be the perfect time for a man to nearly man chat.

"Hey, Con, I know you will be eighteen soon and boys at eighteen are considered to be adults or should have become men by that time. Real men don't usually still live with their mommas. Just know I am looking into housing where you can live on your own as an adult with others of your same kind by then. Let me know if you have any input," Blaze chuckled knowing the unlikeliness of input from his silent son.

The boy continued to stare out the front window but replied, *"On my own pretending he's beside me. All alone, I'll walk with him till morning."*

Such a strange son. Could his head-phoned boy hear or understand what Blaze was saying or was the young man just repeating the song he was listening to? Blaze did not hear the rest of the song that Conifer continue to sing-speak but only in his mind. *"I love him, but every day I'm learning. All my life I've only been pretending. Without me his world will go on turning, a world that's full of happiness that I have never known. I love him but only on my own."*

Chapter 10 notes: Lyrics by Conifer from the *Les Misérables* song *On My Own* by Samantha Barks.

Chapter 11- India 1877

Briary/Mehul

"The Drought -
As the sun dries our grain and crops,
We pray for rain,
But not a single drop.
Our earth is scorched,
Our rivers dry,
Our sheep are thirsty,
And so am I.
With kangaroos dead,
They're put to bed,
But not before,
We've said our prayers.
With each day passing,
Another dies,
And if it keeps going,
So too,
Will you and I."
— Anthony T. Hincks.

Briary lay down utterly exhausted on the straw mattress she and Mehul shared. Her sari wrap hid her emaciated body so well that her loved ones did not know. Briary had been withholding food from herself so there would be enough, or at least more, for her precious son and hardworking husband. They could not carry on their functions to grow and acquire more food without some sustenance, and she was only performing simple chores inside which did not require as much energy. But she was so tired and just needed a little rest, then maybe she could carry on.

The worn straw mattress covered merely by a thin blanket poked through her taut skin, she could feel the jabs in her bones which lay just below the surface. She would be joining the five children that she had lost soon. The thought did not cause her pain; however, she did hate to leave Anoop alone in this harsh world. He would still have Mehul to tend him – good, kind, always sacrificing Mehul. Maybe Mehul would be able to find a Hindu bride to replace her and finally be accepted back into his family. Forgiveness was part of the Hindu dharma. A person who did not forgive was said to be burdened by baggage full of memories of the wrong, on top of negative feelings, anger and unresolved emotions that affected that person's present as well as their future. **Forgiveness was freeing, Briary had forgiven Mehul's family long ago.** She wondered if the Sharma's might even embrace their grandson if she were gone, she prayed so. The people who had raised such a loving son as Mehul certainly could not be cruel enough to reject a motherless child- she hoped.

Briary closed her eyes. She was so thirsty. Heaven sounded peaceful and there must be plentiful amounts of water in heaven. Waterfalls of water cascading all around to gulp down in long drinks… or to bath in… or just float on... even the thought of water washing over her was heavenly. Grandfather John would be there to greet her, and she could finally meet her mother and ask her all of the questions she had held inside since she was a child. Briary pictured her mother as a gloriously beautiful woman with welcoming arms that pulled her daughter close.

Briary was glad she had gotten to see her father one last time and that it had been a positive exchange. If only she had known to say good-bye, but in a world of drought they both realized that every departure could be the last. At his age, Tristan would likely join her and his long-lost bride before long. They could have the family reunion that they were denied here on earth.

There were things Briary had hoped to do before she left, but she did not dwell on them now. Time was flowing together in one big wave. Images of her childhood in the mission intermingled with the births of her own children. She saw herself marrying Mehul, he was standing tall in his colorful traditional dress and she clothed in flowing white holding a wildflower bouquet with more flowers woven through her hair. There she was over the fire stirring a pot of some spiced food that made her dry mouth water just imagining it, next to that scene was a younger Briary who was running free across a field of growing grain with other children her age. Her life swirled around her full of joy and sadness and love and loss. Life was so lovely; she would miss the beauty even with pain and tragedy woven through. The dark patches made the other parts even more vibrant.

Her mother's locket still hung around her thin neck resting above her empty breasts. Briary slipped the chain off over her head and held the small silver heart in her hand, the chain dangling out between her fingers. Mehul had not allowed Briary to sell this keepsake, but she had no daughter to leave it to. She hoped Anoop would treasure it and remember his mother whenever he saw this same necklace that she had worn to remember hers- her silver heart next to his beating one.

Her boys would be back inside soon from attempts to prepare their fallow field for a hopeful crop. They would be expecting a meal. Did she have one last supper in her to give? Could she feed her family with her last breaths? Briary tried to lift her head from the straw mat. When had it become too heavy for her neck to bear? Her slender torso remained pressed down flat against the mat with her legs splayed off the sides of the bed refusing to respond to her commands. Briary closed her eyes one last time and gave in to the darkness.

When Mehul entered their mud-made hut expecting a diminished midday meal, instead, he found no aroma of anything edible in the air. The table was not set, nor any food in sight. On the bed lay his sleeping wife whom he hesitated to wake. It was not like her to sleep during the day so she must truly need her rest. He walked over to her side to gaze at his beloved and lay his hand ever so softly upon his sweet Hiya, she still held his heart and that was the best part of him. She had sacrificed to be with him without so much as a complaint about the hardships they bore. Bearing them together had made their burdens lighter.

Briary's locket slipped from her fingers to the floor. Mehul had never seen his Hiya without the piece of jewelry around her neck. She had offered to sell it for food, but he had refused. It was the one piece of her past she carried with her. Why had she removed it now? Dread filled Mehul. He dropped his head onto his Hiya's chest with an ear over her heart and listened for its reassuring beat. The steady thump

thump de thump so familiar every time he held her close was not present.

He grabbed her shoulders in his calloused hands and drew her body into his arms. There was no need to shake her. Mehul knew immediately she was gone. The spark that gave her life had left. A feral moan that did not sound like it came from within himself escaped Mehul's lips. Of all the losses he had endured over less than four decades of living this one cut him the deepest. If not for Anoop, Mehul would have lain beside his wife and left this world with her. How could he go on? The pain was unbearable. He buried his face in the sari encasing Briary and inhaled the smell of her. He could not let her go.

When Mehul finally lifted his face away from his beloved bride, two greenish-brown eyes looked up questioningly at him. For one so young, his son was far too familiar with death.

Tears glistening on his wet cheeks Anoop asked, "Baba will you build our ma a Taj Mahal?"

With a heart so broken that he had no tears to wet his own face Mehul answered, "I could not bear to have my Hiya anywhere but here near us beta. We will bury your ma with her children- she would like that."

Mehul knew he must keep moving. If he gave in to the grief now, he may never get back up. He brushed his cracked lips ever so gently against his wife's smooth and still slightly warm ones wishing he had captured more kisses in the time they had together. Then he slowly dragged himself to his feet and trudged outside to gather the pick and hoe. He would begin to dig his Hiya's grave immediately. He needed to make a burying place in the brick-hard earth before Briary began to stink. Mehul could give her that one last shred of dignity.

"Baba… should I come… help you dig the hole?" Anoop asked between soundless sobs.

"No beta, you can stay and keep your ma company," Mehul answered. Not only because he wanted to give his son time to grieve his ma, but Mehul also needed time to process his loss alone.

Pick, pick, pick…hoe, hoe, hoe…handfuls of loose dirt. The soil was like stone. Mehul might as well prepare his own resting place while he was at it. His body may still be breathing but all of the good things that made him Mehul had died with his Hiya.

Long absent clouds crept across the graying sky. After a few ceaseless hours of digging, ironic raindrops began to fall on Mehul's damp neck and back giving the barest bit of relief. Perhaps heaven was weeping the tears that Mehul could not for his loss… or finally fulfilling his Hiya's wish for water. The moisture pooled in the cracks between patches of parched ground. Tiny rivers began to run into the shallow grave where Mehul was digging and aided his efforts.

Mehul dug through the night. The rain, even if too late to save his beloved, made his task easier. Even after it stopped, he kept digging, the clouds had passed so he could work by the light of the stars.

In the dawn of early morning, his task complete, Mehul spent and weary, returned to their dwelling. Inside he found Anoop sleeping soundly snuggled next to the body of his dead wife. Hiya's locket hung around Anoop's neck not able to cover the tear streaks that ran through the grime. Mehul did not have the heart to take the token off of the boy. It was Anoop's only inheritance from his ma as it had been Briary's from her own mother. Mehul knew it would not take away the pain but might give some salve in the difficult days to come.

Gently stirring his sleeping son back into his harsh reality Mehul whispered, "Beta, I need you to get up, we have a trip into town today."

Anoop drew himself away from his stiffened mother. Without a word, he shook the sleep from himself and obediently followed his father.

Arriving mindlessly in Agra, without recalling any of the journey they had taken to get there, Mehul knocked on the door of the orphanage where he had first laid eyes on his beloved bride. A plain woman in simple English dress opened the door before them. With kind, but tired eyes that took in the two bedraggled travelers before her, she took Anoop by the hand. Mehul's muddled mind cleared in horror as he realized the woman assumed that he had come to leave the child there as so many others had in the last few months unable to feed their own flesh and blood. If he left Anoop, Mehul would have nothing to live for.

Shaking his head, Mehul spoke, "No, no, may I please speak with your guru or spiritual leader. I have a favor to ask of the man."

As a final act of love and respect Mehul explained to the Christian Guru that he had come to ask him to go back with them and say a few words in the way of a funeral over his wife's grave.

Later that night, after two men from vastly different ideologies and a boy caught between their two worlds, buried the woman they loved, Mehul sat pondering what was next for him and his son. It appeared with the return of the rains, that they might be able to grow a crop again this year. He would trade the rain for the return of his wife, but at least his Anoop should not die now. There was really no place else for them to go except maybe to look for work in the city. And even though Mehul believed that those buried in the ground had gone on to live other lives, it would be hard to leave their precious remains behind in this piece of earth. Mehul removed his turban and climbed into the empty bed knowing that although he was exhausted, sleep would likely not come.

The next day bodies that seemed to have arisen from the dead did appear at his home. Mehul's uncle had heard the news of his Hiya's passing. At his uncle's side were his two brothers and their wives bearing food to share from their scant stores. With added emotion of seeing his lost family before him, Mehul fell to his knees unable to hold back the damn of tears which finally broke spilling wetness from his eyes.

Arjun, the older of his two brothers gently pulled Mehul to his feet and held him upright on unstable legs as he spoke, "Mehul, our baba and ma have also passed in this famine. There has been too much loss. We must reverence the family we have left my brother".

Tears flowing freely, Mehul buried his head in Arjun's shoulder until he could compose himself enough to speak. "Anoop let us welcome our family into our home this day."

The Sharma's would share a solemn celebration marking the end of Briary's life. There would be no crying out or wailing in displays of emotion, but they would be together in their grief and honor the life of the wife they had never met. Perhaps the Waheguru was pleased enough with his Hiya that the two of them had already united and her cycle of birth and death and suffering had ended. In a sorrowful exchange, the loss of his wife had given Mehul back his brothers.

Chapter 10 notes: In Sikh funeral tradition regarding the body, death is a considered natural process of living. It is part of the cycle in Sikhism. This does not apply to the soul, however. The soul uses the body in its journey back to God from where it came. Sikhs prefer cremation over all other ways of disposal. Other methods (including burial in the ground or at sea) are permitted if the cremation is impossible. The cremated remains are typically submerged in a river. The body is just an empty shell to Sikhs. Therefore, there is typically no monument erected for the dead. Crying out, wailing, or other public displays of emotions are disapproved of. Even the closest of relatives try to stay detached from the emotion of the occasion. The body is taken to the place of worship before cremation. There, hymns are sung, and prayers recited. At the site of the cremation, more hymns are sung, and speeches are made about the deceased. At the close, a prayer is said and the youngest son or another close relative will start the cremation. He will either light the fire or start the process mechanically if that is available.

Chapter 12 - Oregon 2020

Conifer

"It's really just the memory of a river.
All waterways have become like phantom limbs.
We might feel that they're still there,
but it's just an illusion cast in cement."
— Jarrod Shusterman, Dry

Conifer was fine that his father returned to New York, but his exit left Conifer thinking about the things the man had said to him in their car ride home. The things that his father did not even think he was smart enough to comprehend. Was his father correct? Did he have no future? Was he a burden? What would he do after high school was over? Could he really get into and go to college? Neem made him believe it was possible, but maybe his dad was right.

Conifer did not think he was stupid. He could understand many things, he just could not get all of the things he knew out of his mouth in a way that other people could understand. Numbers were easy for him. Conifer could do most any mathematical computation in his head, even square roots. And most math problems were completed on paper not vocally which made them easier for him too. Science also seemed completely clear and fell into place in his mind. He could reason out formulas and analyze data for theories without much problem. But when it came time to put that knowledge which was stored in his mind into words that came out from his mouth, there was when the problem occurred.

His dad had a plan for him. Conifer wondered for the hundredth time in less than a day where his dad planned to put him when he turned eighteen. The thought was a little scary and thinking about the unknown made Conifer start clicking his fingers, finger-clicking was one of the nervous tics he was working to control. His dad did not seem nice or mean, just dismissive. His father ignored him and thought he was stupid. Conifer thought a lot, he just could not always make his mouth say the things his brain thought. His thoughts circled and intertwined and overlapped.

Other kids sometimes seemed nice when they were really being mean. And Juniper sometimes seemed angry when she was being nice. She tried to teach him these things, and he knew she was often defending him. It was all so confusing. Conifer needed a computer to calculate emotional input more than he did for math problems. People were far more complicated.

Neem suddenly joined Conifer's mental messiness. Maybe Neem could help him figure out some of these things. Sometimes Neem felt more like a father to him than his own father did.

"Do you think my father is going to lock me away somewhere?" Conifer inquired of his best friend.

"Hopefully not. Your dad is doing his best with what he knows, we will just have to convince him otherwise." Neem cheerfully comforted Conifer.

"Do you think he cares about me at all? I am not sure I fully understand love, but I want him to love me. Aren't fathers supposed to love their sons?" Conifer was not sure why he even cared, but for some reason he did.

"Some people know how to love better than others. Your father has not learned some skills as well as he should have. But parents are precious gifts, and we should appreciate them while we have them." Neem was the precious gift in Conifer's life. He could feel his anxiety start to dissipate with Neem's words.

"How do I make my dad love me. How can I convince him to not send me away?"

"Most people cannot be convinced but have to learn or see the facts for themselves. We both know you have much to offer but we will show your dad too." Neem assured.

"You mean the science project? Can I do a project using my garden or about trees?" Conifer mentally asked.

"Conifer, you definitely have an amazing gift for growing things. We can work with that and maybe expand upon it. Something with even more impact, so the science community cannot ignore the contribution and colleges will be forced to accept you, even fight over you." Neem chuckled at the thought.

Conifer did not like fighting or contention of any kind, but Neem made this fighting sound good. Neem read Conifers thoughts and immediately realigned them.

"Not that kind of fighting Conifer. More like a competition, each college trying to outdo the other's offers to convince you to come to their school. It is a good thing." Neem reassured. "Let's both be thinking. I know we can come up with something that will blow everyone away...but not literally. That just means impress them immensely," Neem clarified for Conifer's literal mind.

Conifer wanted to keep 'talking' with Neem, but Juniper burst into his room and Neem was gone. Neem was hard to hear unless other things were quiet, and his sister was not quiet. She had the dog from her backpack with her. Juniper didn't usually come into his space, he liked to keep his personal area just how he liked it and not have things touched or moved, so he could find what he needed when he needed it. This must be important.

"Conifer, I am sorry to bust in like this, but we need to talk." Was his sister really wanting to talk together or did she mean something else? She did not look happy or sad, but he knew something was not okay. Her energy was palpable. He would just keep listening and hopefully, he would figure out the situation.

"I lied to dad, well I didn't really lie to dad, but I didn't tell him the whole truth. This dog is not for a school project." Juniper admitted. "I just want to figure out the best way to tell mom about Dr. Strange before she finds out he is here. So, will you not say anything until I do? Please."

Conifer was not a huge fan of animals. They were unpredictable, but not more unpredictable than people were and at least they didn't talk. He thought his sister was saying that this dog was going to stay at their house and that it was some kind of doctor…a doctor of strange things. Conifer did not know dogs could be that smart or have those kinds of skills. If a dog could be a doctor, Conifer could certainly go to college. His sister looked so intense and the small hairy doctor did not look like it would be too bad to have around. Conifer felt neutral about the situation but felt he needed to respond.

"You ain't nothin' but a hound dog, cryin' all the time. Well, you ain't never caught a rabbit and you ain't no friend of mine." That is not exactly what he wanted to say.

"Conifer, he doesn't cry much at all, and I think you two could get to be friends." His sister pleaded.

"I love my dog as much as I love you. But you may fade, my dog will always come through." Conifer tried again.

"Well, Conifer, I actually love you more than Dr. Strange. But dogs are loyal. They are supposed to be man's best friend. Do you think you can help me and at least give him a try?" Juniper asked again.

"I guess I just didn't know little boys grow up and dogs get old." It was the best dog lyric than came to Conifer's mind. Even he knew it didn't make total sense, but hopefully, his sister would understand that he was willing to let the dog stay and grow old.

"Ahh my bestest-bro, I knew you would come through. I will tell mom soon I promise. And I think you are going to love this little guy." In response, the dog licked his sister's face.

Conifer did not like the name bro at all even if he was the best one, and he certainly did not want the dog licking any of his body parts. But Juniper rarely used the name and the dog had done nothing but look at him with its big brown and blue eyes. Although he was not usually comfortable in new situations this one could be okay. He must have somehow reassured his sister enough since she and the dog bounded from his room. Maybe he could do a science project about dogs…no, probably not. That would take more research than he was willing to do on the subject, but he was willing to give his sister's canine a try. After all, Juniper had told him that Dr. Strange was man's best friend, even though Conifer believed with all of his heart that Neem was his best friend- always and forever.

Chapter 12 notes: There is currently no medical detection or cure for autism spectrum disorder. Parents do not and cannot cause autism spectrum disorder although the multiple causes of ASD are not known. Individuals with autism spectrum disorder have communication deficits. ASD is not degenerative and individuals with ASD can continuously improve. They are most likely to improve through early intervention with specialized, individualized services and opportunities for supported inclusion. Being nonverbal at age 4 does not mean children with autism spectrum disorder will never speak. Research shows that most will learn to use words and nearly half will learn to speak fluently.

Conifer's song lyrics- *Hound Dog* by Elvis Presley, *I Love my Dog* by Cat Stevens, and *Little Boys Grow Up and Dogs get Old* by Luke Bryant.

Chapter 13 – Oregon 2020

Juniper

*"We tend to take summer's vitality for granted,
when in actuality it is just one prolonged drought,
or disease, away from decimation."*
— Sue Leaf, *The Bullhead Queen: A Year on Pioneer Lake*

What impeccably poor timing Dr. Strange had to reveal his presence to her father of all people. The initial moment had been intense, but Blaze had left without blowing Dr. Strange's cover to her mother. That was more than she could have hoped for, it must have slipped his mind. She did not see her padre as a guy who normally showed much mercy. Conifer seemed cool about it. She was pretty sure he wouldn't tell their mom and if he tried to, she could interpret his lyrics to lean in her favor. But summer break was nearly upon them and Juniper didn't want to keep the dog stuffed under her bed all summer. The little guy should be running around outside and traipsing through the garden like Peter Cottontail. Conifer wasn't really a Mr. McGregor-type, but he definitely wouldn't be happy to have a dog romping among his master gardening. The imagined chaos that could ensue made her smile.

She needed to tell her mother about their new tenant and the sooner the better. Maybe the news would come best via a text. No, that would be too impersonal to touch her mom's heart. A letter of written explanation may be better. Oh, and she could pin the note to the darling puppy dropped off on their front porch. Not that Juniper was afraid of her mom, she was a teddy bear compared to her dad, but an abandoned baby of any species would tug on her mom's heartstrings and make adoption more likely.

Juniper grabbed a pen and nondescript piece of paper and began to write the message in all capitals to disguise her handwriting. She chuckled at the idea of cutting out the letters from a magazine like they did in ransom notes but that might be a bit creepy and would take too long. Juniper began to write: "I WAS DROPPED OFF ON THE SIDE OF THE ROAD AND ALL MY SIBLINGS ARE GONE. COULD YOU PLEASE TAKE ME IN AND LOVE ME?" Perhaps a tad dramatic, but hopefully effective.

Her mother would be back from her AA meeting soon. Not Alcoholic Anonymous, but Juniper liked to tease her mom that Autism Awareness had the same acronym. Juniper needed to work fast to have things ready for when Mumsie got home. She slid the box cradling the darling dog out from under her bed and switched the tell-tale blanket out for some paper towels. The towels looked bleaker and her mom would recognize her blankie. She gave Dr. Strange a quick clean up but did not want him to look too tended to, just not disease-caring dirty. He was patient with her eye wiping and gentle brushing and was now ready for the show.

Before long Brooke entered the house carrying the boxed dog in her arms which Juniper took to be a good sign. "Look what I found on our doorstep. Poor little guy. Someone must have known you work at the dog rescue, Junie."

Dang, Juniper had not thought through that option. "Maybe mom, or maybe they just know what a great nurturer you are and thought we would make a good home for him." She shouldn't have added the gender of the dog. How could she have known it was a 'him' from across the room? But her mom missed the slip-up.

"Juniper, you know I have said no dogs, for many reasons." Her mom reminded while glancing across the room towards Conifer, "but this puppy is pretty cute."

There, a tiny window of 'maybe' was opening. How could any sane and decent person resist a puppy? "Mom, I have a good feeling that Conifer is going to be okay with the dog. Can we at least give it a trial run for a few days and see how things go before you send him off to institutionalized care? The dog, not Conifer." That should get to Brooke, her mother hated having anyone that was challenged with special needs institutionalized.

"Perhaps we can give the dog one week, just seven days, but if it doesn't work out for any reason you must promise to take him directly to the rescue." Brooke compromised.

So, Dr. Strange would be here on probation. Juniper could live with that. However, she did wonder how long before the guilt from the charade would get to her and she would have to confess the truth of her furry friend's arrival to her mother. Hopefully, not for over seven days at least.

"Thanks so much, mom, it will go great, you will see. I am thinking Dr. Strange may be the perfect name for him. The little guy looks intelligent in a strange way and you have always wanted a doctor in the family." Juniper grinned.

Her mom returned the smile. "Sounds like you have this all figured out; we will see. Just go slow with your brother and don't let the dog upset him."

There was an interrupting knock at the front door. Juniper had texted her brilliant plan to Stetson and he said he would drop by for backup if needed.

"I'll get it." Juniper offered, hurrying to update Stetson before he over-did the schmoozing.

"Dog-relocation-support at your service. Will convince anyone, anywhere, that they need a canine in their life." Stetson entered in salesman mode.

"Shhhh, I already have that under control. Let's say you are here for another driving lesson instead." Juniper whispered.

But Stetson insisting on tormenting her for a minute first, he had come prepared and was not going to drop the dog topic immediately, "Mrs. Ridgeway what do you have in that box? A puppy, no way, I haven't seen a dog like that one at the shelter. I wonder where he could have come from. Looks like the perfect breed for a family dog." Stetson sent an impish grin Juniper's way. "And if it would it be alright; could I give your daughter another driving lesson?"

Her mother agreed to let Juniper go driving and didn't even make her take Conifer or the dog. Either her mom was relieved to have Stetson take a turn or else Dr. Strange was already working his puppy magic on momma Brooke.

Juniper headed to the passenger side of Stetson's Impala before he stopped her, "Hey, get over here to this side of the car and get behind the wheel like a regular driving student, it is time for some real road experience for you."

Not really sure that she was ready, Juniper obeyed her teacher's orders and followed all the pre-driving instructions he had given her the last time before backing out of the driveway.

"Great start, my star pupil." Stetson joked.

"It helps that I am your only pupil unless you are running a driving school somewhere on the side that I am unaware of. Where are we going?" Juniper asked.

"First a little downtown driving and then either the highway or some rural roads where you can give it a little gas, but not as much as at the track, please. I don't have a driving instructor's safety brake on my side like in the real training cars." Stetson warned.

They wove through a few city streets that were not too busy, working on stoplights, stop signs, yields and staying in her own lane. Stetson's major critiques were about not stopping so close to the car in front of her and giving herself enough time to brake smoothly. She did slam on the brakes a few times throwing them both forward, but Stetson was extremely patient, and no shrieks of fright were involved like when her mother supervised.

When he finally felt comfortable with her in-town efforts, Stetson had Juniper head north on Shevlin Park Road towards the park that the road was named after. Shevlin Park

114

was only a few miles from Bend and Juniper had spent time there with her family hiking, nature exploring and even fishing in the pond, but she had never caught any fish. As they pulled into the parking lot Juniper was relieved that the drive hadn't been stressful. The two had gotten to know each other a little better and laughed at her rookie mistakes.

"Time for an intermission break, go ahead and put the car in park." Stetson directed.

Juniper was getting ready to hop out when she noticed Stetson was easing his way closer to her on the old bench seat. Where were bucket seats when you needed them? Now opening the car door might appear like an attempt to escape. She had absolutely no experience in this arena, even less than she did with driving, and Juniper was positive she would make a mess of whatever happened next.

"Gosh Juni-per, you look more freaked out than when we were in heavy traffic. Relax, I am not going to attack you. I think you are amazing and have wanted to kiss you for a long time. If that isn't okay, I promise I won't, but it might be better than you think." Stetson gave her his irresistible smile and waited for her response.

Either way the drive home was bound to be awkward now and he definitely did look kissable. "I must warn you that I am probably pretty bad at it since I have never kissed anyone before," Juniper admitted. "Well, besides my mom on the cheek and a few dogs if those count."

"That's hard to believe, but I would be honored to get your first real kiss and hope to not end up in the dog category," Stetson looked hopeful.

Juniper thought most boys just went in for it and were not so respectful as to ask permission first, she had to give the guy props for that. Without saying anything else that would put even more pressure on the moment she slid closer to Stetson and shut her eyes puckering her lips like she had seen in a movie.

Stetson's warm hand cupped the back of her neck, probably so she couldn't pull away, and he placed his other hand on the side of her check softly tilting her head a smidge. It felt like he had practiced this maneuver before, but she didn't want to think about that. The smell of spearmint gum or breath mint caught her nose before his lips actually connected with hers. Their lips didn't actually lock together, but there was a definite connection of nerve endings firing off as Stetson's lips pressed gently against hers. It was as if his lips were waiting patiently for a reply. Juniper feared that she would have no idea what to do next, but her lips had a mind of their own and responded anyway. She was pretty sure that she was an awful kisser, but she did at least kiss him back and didn't leave those alluring lips hanging.

As they pulled apart Stetson asked, "Now that wasn't so terrible was it?"

"Not for me, but probably for you," Juniper honestly answered.

"Not bad, not bad at all." Stetson teased, "and I am sure we can practice more in the future, but one lesson at a time. I better get you home so I can keep in your mother's good graces."

Instead of getting out of the car he reached across her to grab the steering wheel and lifted himself over her into the driver's seat. It was getting dark, so she was glad he was going to drive. Neither spoke much on the drive home. In front of her house Juniper jumped out of the car after thanking Stetson for the driving lesson while wondering if he was serious about giving her kissing lessons too.

"My pleasure Miss Juni-per Ridgeway. Have a great night and I'll see you at the Rescue tomorrow. Hope you can convince your mom to keep the dog." Then Stetson Buttars casually drove off into the sunset.

The house was quiet when she entered, even Dr. Strange was asleep in his box. Juniper was a long way from ready for sleep. Her mind was buzzing with her first kiss on top of everything else that had happened that day. Maybe she had finally caught a fish at Shevlin Park after all. She picked up her laptop and sat down on the couch. Not much into social media, she opened the family search website to cruise around until she settled down enough to go to bed.

The Ridgeway line was still a dead end. Juniper would be so excited when she finally found some relatives of her father's. She would appreciate any tidbit of information that might help her connect in some way to the man living in New York who was supposedly her biological dad. She kept trying to find something they might have in common that would create a bond. For now, she returned to the Fountain side of the family. Her brain could not handle much more excitement tonight, but it was fun to learn that her ancestors had lived in Great Britain in the early 1800s. She was researching information about the children of her seventh great grandparents who had lived in the town of Sheffield a borough in South Yorkshire, England.

Albert and Anna Fountain had given birth to eight children, only four of whom lived past infancy according to their death dates. How hard that must have been on her many-times-great grandma Anna. William, Walter, Thomas, Edward, Albert, and John were their sons. Anna and Katherine were their daughters. Juniper wondered what had become of all these people, four of which had lived lives walking, talking, living and breathing on this earth just like she did. She checked the 1800 census and some gravestone and obituary sites. Genealogy was like unraveling a tangled mystery with many missing pages.

It was getting late when she found an entry for Anna K. Fountain who died in 1808. Juniper read in what was likely her ancestor's obituary that her son John was serving as a missionary in India when she died. Crazy, Juniper's many-times-great uncle had moved to India. She wondered if they still had family members who lived in the Far East. Now Juniper had even more circling in her mind to keep her awake, but the major question that loomed in her congested brain was if Stetson was thinking about her tonight too? She lay on her bed with Dr. Strange who no longer had to hide beneath it and shut her eyes curious about what or who would be in her dreams.

Chapter 13 notes: I was unable to find details about John Fountain's family who remained back in Great Britain, so the information about his family and their location is fictional. I chose the town of Sheffield because the name means "river sheaf" which goes with the book's theme. And there really is a Shevlin Park in Bend, Oregon

Chapter 14 - India 1895-1896

Anoop

"The exhausted earth groaned and quivered under the monotonous glare of the sun. Spirals of heat rose from the ground as if from molten lava. A panting lizard crawled painfully over the fevered rock in search of a shady crevice. Cattle and dogs cringed under the scanty shade of the trees and waited for the rain to deliver them from the heat and thirst. Instead the heat grew more intense and oppressive each day, singeing and stifling all living things with an invisible sheet of fire, which only the rain could put out. The drought had persisted for over a month."
— S. Rajaratnam, *The Short Stories and Radio Plays of S. Rajaratnam*

The sky was clear with no wisp of a cloud in sight, and rays of heat shimmered off the baked clay soil. Anoop recalled this same extreme dryness during the agonizing year that they lost his mother. Hopefully, both of his parent's God would not let this drought take away more of those he loved. Anoop wondered if his mother had any influence over the weather now that she was closer to its source. He certainly had no control, nor did his baba. Padma dealt with the crisis very well for one so young and that was a blessing. She was not like his own mother, but few women in India were. Padma offered Anoop support, a stable life and she was carrying another life that would soon be added to their home. Anoop placed his hand over his wife's swollen belly. He was growing to care more each day for this strong woman whom he had been given the choice to take as his bride. Theirs may not be as powerful as his parent's love story, but they would create their own.

Mehul and Anoop had stayed on their land and harvested a meager crop the year after his ma had died. Each year had been a little better until this past harvest. At one-point, Anoop had considered leaving the farm to become a soldier like his grandpa Tristan. Soldiering was an honorable profession in India, and the British used India's manpower as the backbone of their military power. Soldiers always got fed and Anoop could escape the memories of his hard life and of the others who had lost theirs here on the farm. But in the end, he could not leave his baba alone. After his soldiering-crossroads decision, Anoop became one hundred percent committed to staying on the farm and working to make their land productive enough to sustain their two lives as well as whoever else joined them in the future. He had finally given up on his goal of doing something wonderful, his main plan now was to survive.

Mehul never remarried. His father said that his true heart had been buried with his Hiya. The one that remained beating in his chest kept him alive, but it could not love another woman in her place. Mehul wanted Anoop to find the same kind of love that he had shared with Anoop's ma, but it was difficult in their world. Where would Anoop find her? In the end, Mehul had arranged a suitable match for his son, but with Anoop's input and permission.

Padma was from Agra and her family belonged to a slightly lower caste which had not mattered to the Sharma's. Anoop's mixed blood, as well as religious views, had mattered to some of the others in the village, but not to Padma's parents who were also followers of the Sikh faith. The newlyweds had married in a traditional Hindu ceremony, his bride dressed in red with a bindi on her forehead and hands painted with a henna design. In memory of his ma, Anoop made sure to add a few Christian touches. The couple exchanged simple wedding bands after their seven vows in Sanskrit were spoken, and a wedding cake was served with the usual wedding meal. Anoop still wore his mother's locket around his neck with a small cross that he had etched into the silver on the backside. In his heart, he hoped that his mother had been able to watch from wherever she was, and the few Christian customs he added in her honor made him feel like she was there.

Before the wedding, Anoop and his baba built an extra room onto the family house to make space for his bride and their future family that would hopefully come one day. Mehul could not be expected to climb the ladder to Anoop's loft at his age, so Mehul kept the same bedroom that he had shared with his wife and they built another sleeping room on the opposite side of the home for Anoop and his new spouse. The multi-generational family would share the common area between, and Padma now cooked and tended to both men, but in different ways.

Padma was a combination of tender and tough and she taught Anoop things about life that he could not have imagined. The pregnancy had come soon after the marriage and had been a surprise to them both. Padma was not as fragile as his mother, but Anoop made sure she had enough to eat for both herself and the child. This drought was not as severe as the last, but water had been scarce, and food limited. Anoop thought of his less than reluctant bride as he worked side by side with his aging father to gather the scant crop again this year. He did care for Padma deeply, perhaps he even loved her already. Anoop's treks to visit his buried siblings had grown less and less as he was able to visit with a flesh and blood woman who could discuss the matters of his mind and heart returning conversation and answering him back in reply.

The evening was calm and not too warm as the three Sharma's finished their supper meal of ground jowar and lightly spiced dal. Padma did not use seasonings as well as ma yet, but her food was satisfying.

"I believe it's time," Padma said softly as pain contorted her plain face.

Mehul knew instantly what the girl meant and jumped to his feet. "Anoop, comfort your wife while I go to town for help." His father offered.

"Please bring my ma to me if you can," Padma intensely requested in her quiet tone.

Anoop felt afraid. His father would know better what to do should the baby come; Mehul should be the one staying here. Anoop should be the one going into town. But one look into Padma's panicked eyes and he knew he could not leave her. This woman bearing his child was even more afraid than he was and needed him to help her through. "Yes baba, go get help. Hurry to get back before the baby comes," Anoop pleaded.

"Don't worry beta. The first birth takes longer than those that will follow. I will be back before the child arrives."

Mehul assured over his shoulder as he had already begun the journey.

Anoop knew nothing about birthing, they had not even had animals he could watch in nature's cycle of reproduction. However, he did know something about comforting another human being. He and his father had taken turns comforting one another through the darkest days of their lives. Turning one's mind from the sorrow had helped most. Anoop had learned to be a master storyteller to take his father away from his grief when he could no longer bear it.

Sitting on the bed where this painful situation had begun, Anoop drew the shoulders of his petite olive-skinned wife back against his chest to support her back while she sat between his legs and begun to tell her a story as he gently rubbed her contracting abdomen to help relax the tension. He had no idea if this was the right thing to do, he could be making things worse, but he could feel the muscles in Padma's back relax between the labor pains as she laid her head back on his chest.

"Once there was a beautiful young girl born into a country that was not really hers." Anoop began as Padma's breathing became heavy and jagged. "Her mother welcomed her into the world and then left it herself." Smooth move, Anoop mentally lashed himself. He should not be bringing up death in childbirth at a time like this, even if it was a very real occurrence. "The girl grew up very loved and surrounded by angels who taught her how to love too. One day a man from another world saw this lovely creature of light and had to bring her home so that he could partake of the light as well."

Padma moaned as pain gripped her body pulling her belly tight around the baby balled inside. "Please tell me more husband," she requested through pursed lips with her eyes closed.

Anoop knew this was not one of his better stories, but he kept going. "The man and woman became one in every purpose that this life had to offer them and brought six children into the world in a very short time."

"Is this the story of your own parents?" Padma asked as she stifled a scream gulping for air.

"Somewhat," Anoop admitted. "Theirs has always been the greatest love story I know, and I have always hoped to have my own like theirs one day." Watching his bride struggle in pain to give them a child of their own, Anoop's heart swelled within him and he realized that he did love this woman dearly. "I am here my Hiya, I am here. Would you rather I tell you the story of the Taj Mahal?" Could he not think of a story where the woman in childbirth lived? Anoop continued sharing stories while attempting to ease Padma's physical discomfort until finally, he heard footsteps outside.

His baba with Padma's frantic ma returned to relieve the depleted new husband only shortly before a tiny pink body was squeezed forth into the world. Anoop did not know if he had ever seen anything more beautiful. Once his mother-in-law made sure the baby had all ten fingers and toes, she swaddled the squalling child and presented Anoop with his infant daughter. Anoop's heart swelled to near bursting with the surge of love he felt for this itsy-bitsy being. Padma had done well; he was so proud of both of his girls.

Tenderly bending down, Anoop showed his exhausted bride the precious bundle that he clutched protectively and going against tradition asked, "Can we call her Briary Padma Sharma?"

Chapter 14 notes: India was the jewel in the crown of the British Empire. As well as spices, jewels, and textiles, India had a huge population. Soldiering was an honorable tradition in India and the British capitalized on this. They regimented India's manpower as the backbone of their military power.

Hindu weddings last three days and include the items mentioned in this chapter as well as many more. Red is considered in India as the symbol of prosperity and fertility, it also signifies the color of love and strength. Therefore, most Hindu and Sikh brides wear red-colored attire for their wedding since it signifies these important aspects of their lives. A Hindu marriage joins two individuals for life, so that they can pursue *dharma* (duty), *artha* (possessions), *kama* (physical desires), and *moksha* (ultimate spiritual release) together.

Chapter 15 – New York 2020 and 1977

Blaze

Violence is like a weed - it does not die even in the greatest drought. - Simon Wiesenthal

Blaze leaned back in the leather chair behind his desk remembering the fighting words his daughter had flung at him before he left Oregon, claiming that his ancestors were "invisible or non-existent". Of course, neither was true, but his concern was that this girl was smart enough to find them and the truth. His name change should keep her off their scent for some time and possibly forever, but he could not be sure. The girl had no idea that he was protecting her as well as himself by hiding their pedigree chart. She needed to leave the past alone, keep it buried deep in ambiguity, that would be best for everyone involved.

He had been born Dick Minor which was a long way from Blaze Ridgeway. Blaze had considered merely becoming Richard Major, just a slight variation to a more powerful version of his name but decided it would be too easy to track. No, he was blazing a totally new trail for himself and planned to make it to the top of the mountain looking down on those who had belittled him, so Blaze Ridgeway was a fitting moniker for an up and coming financial mogul. It had been so amazingly easy and inexpensive to legally change his whole name that he was surprised more people didn't do it.

Kylie knocked on his door before pushing it open, obviously not feeling the need to ask for permission to enter but at least giving him a heads up.

"Yes, what is it?" Blaze asked with an edge to his voice even though it was evident he was not busy and that she was not interrupting anything.

"I just have a couple of questions for you about the Severson and Kaufman portfolios. I caught a couple red of flags; the numbers aren't adding up," ever efficient Kylie suggested.

Being surrounded by bright women was not always a blessing in his life. Why did they look further than they needed to into his business? "Thank you, just leave the files on my desk and I will have a look," Blaze responded more casually than he felt, trying to keep things cool.

"Here, let me show you what looks off to me," Kylie offered stepping forward with the paperwork in hand.

"I said just leave them," Blaze repeated more sternly. He was not ready or in the mood to deal with another crisis at the moment.

Kylie gave him a perturbed look but set down the files and backed from his office. Blaze should have handled that much better. Instead of defusing the situation, he had thrown gasoline on it. He hoped he was not going to have to let the girl go, she was good, too good for her own good it appeared. Blaze sighed as his thoughts returned to his ancestor issue.

Last that he knew, he had a mother and sister living in Malone, New York, but that was over twenty years ago. He was pretty sure his father, Bobby Minor, was still there too. Not living at home with Blaze's mom, but in the Upstate Correctional Facility located in the same town. Upstate Correctional was a super-max security state prison for inmates with a history of assaultive behavior. Yes, that was dear ole dad's home if he was still alive. Bobby Minor was serving thirty years to life for aggravated assault with a deadly weapon. He had shot a man during an armed robbery. The family had moved to Malone to be near Bobby for visitation days.

Pretty much everything Blaze remembered about his life as Dickie Minor was awful and pathetic. He had been teased horribly for his poor haircut, holey shoes with cutout pieces of cardboard in the soles and ill-fitting hand-me-down clothes that their welfare case manager provided. His mom and little sister were so meek and beaten down it didn't seem to bother them as much, but his whole pre-Blaze existence was cringe worthy. He had an afterschool job stocking shelves at the market and his mom did laundry and mending. She had virtually no other skills and by taking in clothing items she could be home with his baby sister. Between welfare and their two supplemental incomes the three of them did not starve, but by the time he hit junior high even the free lunches were an embarrassment.

The final straw came on the day a fellow student came up to him pointing out a greasy spot on his shirt and saying that Dickie's mother had missed it when washing their family's clothes. That was it. Blaze, better known as Dickie back then, blew a fuse and let loose a punch that connected with the cocky boy's nose. As blood from the blow dripped through fingers covering the boy's now probably broken nose, he shouted that Dickie was just like his father and would end up in Upstate Correctional himself one day. The reality of the accusation turned Dickie inside out and upside down. He would not stay living in the shadow of the prison being reminded daily of all that he was not or what he might become.

Dickie had read stories of boys running off and joining the circus, he wondered if they still existed. He had never been to one. He stuffed a change of clothes into a sack and then realizing he had nothing of worth to take with him, Dickie left Malone without saying goodbye to even his mother. He doubted he would be missed, except for the few dollars his meager paycheck brought in, his mom would likely be relieved to have one less mouth to feed. A trucker going south gave Dickie a ride to the city and he had been in NYC ever since.

The first few years had been rough. Living on the streets, he found a job washing dishes and snuck into men's restrooms, covered doorway entrances or dark forgotten corners of pubs to sleep when it got cold. The nightlife in the city never closed down so there was always someplace open. He was tall for his age and could grow a few scraggly whiskers by fourteen, so no one realized how young he really was.

A dishwashing job turned into a busboy position and then one as a waiter and after a few years, he was able to get a cheap room across the river in Jersey. He picked up as many shifts a week as the manager would allow and learned all he could from the tables he worked by observing and listening. The best dressed and best tipping customers seemed to be from the financial district, so that is what Dickie, now Blaze, had decided he would become a financial advisor or stockbroker.

Dickie knew he was smart and if Frank Abagnale, Jr. (the guy from the movie *Catch Me if you Can*) could work as a doctor, a lawyer, and as a co-pilot for a major airline -- all before his eighteenth birthday, Blaze could certainly figure out his way into the world of finance. He forged a bachelor's degree from a minor university that no one would care about and started studying his new field of desired knowledge. He frequented the library where he could find resource books on finance and gain online access to more in-depth information until he could eventually afford his own laptop computer.

There was too much security and thorough background checks to get a job on the floor of the stock exchange but to become a stockbroker only required a bachelor's in business administration. Blaze could become a licensed professional who advised clients and managed their investments in stocks, bonds, and other securities. He discovered that a license wasn't required to trade stocks in your own brokerage account, so Blaze had his foot firmly in the door of the club he sought access to.

Blaze began to study everything he could find about the stock market and he practiced investing in market trends with imaginary money. He learned that the single biggest reason most traders failed to make money was lack of knowledge and he was not going to let that happen. More importantly, he structured and implemented strong money management rules before he began, such as stop-loss and position sizing measures to ensure minimal risk and maximum profits since he had no money to lose. His biggest break came by sheer luck when he invested most of his real money into a couple of stocks that happened to hit the big time shortly afterward.

In 1996 Blaze noticed in the Wall Street Journal that the coffee he liked, called Green Mountain Coffee Roasters had stock selling cheap on NASDAQ for only twenty-three cents a share. On a whim, or maybe more a gut and palate hunch, he took a chance on it, acquiring a thousand shares for only a little over two hundred dollars. He also picked up a bundle of Apple stock shares which had been a well-known computer company in the 1970s and 1980s before experiencing a decline. In 1996, Apple's shares were trading below a dollar at only ninety-one cents apiece.

No one imagined that by 2016 GMCR shares of Green Mountain Coffee (then Keurig Green Mountain) would be trading for $89.86 per share, multiplying his initial investment by nearly four hundred times. The company was now Keurig Dr. Pepper, combining with another popular beverage company should only increase its value even more. Then after successfully designing and marketing popular products, such as the iPod, MacBook, iPhone, and iPad, along with software such as iTunes and the App Store, his Apple shares by 2016 were worth $93.99 apiece. Increasing his Apple investment by over one hundred times as well, not the home run his coffee stock had given him, but not too shabby of a return for a day in the office.

Blaze wished he had been able to purchase ten times the amount of stock that he had back then, but the proceeds and dividends had enabled him to not only establish his own business, but he gained a substantial base of clients along the way mainly due to selecting those major market growth companies. He added Netflix and Amazon to his portfolio before they became best-performers and Blaze became known as a blazing wizard on Wall Street. Playing the market had been easier than striking gold.

Brooke entered his life shortly after he became established in his new career. Before then having a permanent woman around would have been a hindrance and only distracted Blaze from his success. He hadn't wanted any tell-tale remnants of his past lingering around when he found an eventual wife. Blaze had become the man he wanted the world to see and finally buried Dickie far behind in his past.

Ridgeway Elevated Financial Services sporting a mountain ridge logo had even survived the market crash of 2008 and come out clean with its head above water. If Blaze hadn't become impatient along the way (he could not admit even to himself the word greedy) and started some more creative moves with his finances, he would be living the high life without the extra stresses pressing down on him right now. Well, without his business stresses anyway. There was still the stressful family situation out in Oregon. He had already left one family behind in Upstate New York only to create another family with different issues. Perhaps he should have remained a lone wolf. The Wolf of Wall Street had a nice ring to it too.

That reminded him, Blaze pressed the intercom, "Kylie, can you come back in for a moment please?"

The attractive assistant stepped back into his office, "Did you find the problems I am talking about. Can you explain to me why the numbers are so off? What am I missing?"

Time to misdirect the girl's focus and take care of another problem at the same time. "I haven't had a chance to go over the portfolios yet. I was just checking back on what information you were able to find for me on adult living institutions." Blaze inquired.

"Yes, I have that in the other room, it would have been easier if I had been given a more specific client to be looking for, but I found a few possible locations for generic situations. Let me go get them." Kylie exited to complete the task. She would hopefully forget about the Severson and Kaufman accounts in the process- not likely knowing her. Blaze's concerns were stacking up like the wooden blocks in a game of Jenga and it was just a matter of time before one of the blocks was going to fall and make his whole tower tumble. Somehow, he needed to rebuild the teetering tower. There was no way he was ever going back to his former status of existence.

Chapter 15 notes: The information about stock-brokering as well as the Apple and Green Mountain Coffee Roasters stocks is all accurate.

Chapter 16 – India 1948

Anoop

"I cared for you in the wilderness, In the land of drought" -
Hosea 13:5

Anoop heard each breathe rattle in his chest and knew it would not be long before he drew his last. He had lived a fine life, an extremely long life from India standards, but he was tired and ready to go wherever the next step through death's door took him. Unfortunately, he had accomplished nothing of an impressive nature in his eight decades on earth. Anoop felt like he had let his siblings down with his failed efforts to honor their deaths. He had not been able to do something wonderful in acknowledgment of their short lives. But he could not call his life a total failure.

He had been a devoted son, tending to his father until they buried Mehul's ashes next to his Hiya in the family plot nearly thirty years ago. Anoop had been a faithful husband who loved his arranged-marriage wife as if she had been born of his heart. Padma still stood by his side in her aging years serving him well with her better health. She would continue on when he was gone, their youngest son stood by her side like Anoop had supported his own baba.

His three living children, two of which now surrounded him in anticipation of his big sendoff, had grown up to be decent human beings contributing positive energy to the world. He and Padma had only lost one of their babies in infancy due to the harshness of living. His older son Reyansh, named after Anoop's only brother, had come to visit him during the previous week but had now returned to Delhi for work after Anoop lingered longer than expected. Younger Reyansh had always possessed a studious nature that was not conducive to contentment on the farm. The boy attended the university in Delhi, studied there and then stayed to be a doctor. His family had electricity and running water in their home. Anoop and Padma visited the city-dwelling Sharma's in Delhi once several years ago. Congested city living was not for him, but his eldest son was a success by the world's measurements.

Their only living daughter, Briary Padma, married a distant cousin from Jaipur and moved to the 'pink city' as it was called due to the many buildings painted that color in honor of Queen Victoria's visit. His daughter lived there with her husband's family but came to Agra every year to see Anoop and Padma. Briary looked more like her mother than the grandmother she was named after but carried in her nature the best parts of both women. She was a loving daughter and was here now to support her ma and say goodbye to her baba. Anoop cherished his gentle girl.

His youngest son, who shared his name but was called Noopi to avoid confusion, had stayed with his parents on the farm. He and his arranged wife moved into Mehul's room after his dada had passed and they shared their home and their labors like baba Anoop had before him. Both Anoop's would live on in this soil and in the memories of this land even after buried in it.

His breath gurgled in the back of his throat. Anoop had survived two droughts but ironically his lungs were now drowning in fluid. Reyansh using his medical diagnosis and terminology had called it pneumonia. It appeared Anoop's God was calling him home or would be sending him on another assignment soon.

He would miss the nine grandchildren that would be left behind to carry on his legacy. Five of them were Sharma's so the family name would not die with him which was an odd comfort at this time. Padma lifted his head from the pillow. "Have a drink husband, you will rest easier." Anoop did not feel thirsty but obliged his helpful Padma. The water he could not swallow drained out the side of his mouth and rolled to the back of his neck dampening the pillow.

"Baba, can I change your pillow or roll you on your side to give your back a rub?" Briary, his mini-Padma, offered.

"I am good my daughter," Anoop lied or at least covered the whole truth. "Thank you."

"He just needs to rest," Noopi suggested. "All is well on the farm baba; the crop is growing well this year. We will have a good harvest." Those were the things that a man believed would bring the most comfort. He did not want his father to worry. Noopi would take care of the family when Anoop was gone.

Padma, never one for public displays of affection took Anoop's calloused hand, spotted from years in the sun, into her own and pressed her cheek to it tenderly. Anoop knew by the simple gesture that his family knew that he was dying. A tear from the corner of his eye dripped onto his wife's gnarled fingers, beading up before falling to the floor.

"You are a fine woman Padma. We have been blessed all these years..." Anoop did not have much energy to speak and even these few words threw him into a coughing spasm.

"The grandchildren are waiting outside; can I bring them for a few minutes? Would you like to say hello?" Padma asked, certainly realizing it was more of a goodbye, but not speaking the obvious.

Anoop nodded his head, saving his words for the young ones. Five or maybe six young bodies paraded past his bed bowing to give their dada a hug and then waited for him to say something. What words could he say for them to remember him by? What would make any difference? He knew that there was not much they would be able to change in the world, but he wanted to leave them with hope.

"Love one another…be there for one another… family is the most important thing. Know wherever I am I will be watching over you. You will always be loved." There was much more he wanted to say. Much more that he should say. He looked from face to face, tears welled up in one of the little one's eyes, blank stares came from another, and a frightened expression from the third as Briary led the crew out of the room. What would their India look like?

Anoop was leaving his family to live in a free India. He had not imagined he would live to see this day, that was an accomplishment. Hopefully, his children's and grandchildren's lives would be better than his had been and they would cherish their independence. Just last year the

British House of Commons passed the Indian Independence Act and divided India into two regions - India and Pakistan. Their attempt to solve the religious unrest by having the Muslims live in Pakistan and the Hindu stay in India had not gone as planned so far. Most inhabitants of India were against the split and there was even more contention and upheaval instead of less.

Mahatma Gandhi was trying to mend the anger between the two sides by advocating non-violence between the groups. Gandhi was exactly the same age as Anoop, but Mahatma had spent his whole life making a difference with his civil movement against British rule. Gandhi had done more with the same number of days that he had been given. He had transformed the Indian National Congress from an elite group to a party of mass appeal. Yet Gandhi's end was not as peaceful as Anoop's. He had not been surrounded by his family during his final hours. When Anoop's eldest son came from Delhi last week to look in on his father's health, he shared the sad news that Gandhi had been killed. The non-violent ambassador had been assassinated by one of his own fanatic followers.

Why would a man who had done so much good be shot by one of his own people? Anoop shut his eyes slightly shaking his head at the thought and realized that his life had been pretty wonderful. He was encircled by love and no one wanted to shoot him. And who was to say he was not leaving as much as Gandhi had to the world? It was for the future to determine what the family he was leaving behind would yet contribute. One of his descendants may leave a mark as deep as Mr. Mahatma himself. Anoop's favorite saying or inspired message from Gandhi was that "Your life is your message." What message had Anoop left for his family?

Anoop could still hear his family's conversation in the background, but he felt his reality shifting to another dimension.

"Reyansh?" Anoop fitfully called out.

"Baba, Reyansh isn't here," Briary comforted. "But we are here."

"Yes, yes, Reyansh is here…" Anoop spoke his last words as he took ahold of his glorious brother's hand and walked through the door with him to find out for himself what came next.

Chapter 16 notes: On June 15, 1947, the British House of Commons passed the Indian Independence Act or Mountbatten Plan, which divided India into two dominions, India and Pakistan. It called for each dominion to be granted its independence by August 15th of that year. The Indian independence movement took place from 1857 until August 1947, when India got independence from the British Raj. The movement spanned a total of 90 years. Before 1947, there were two types of states present in India - princely states and provincial states. At the time of the British withdrawal, 565 princely states were officially recognized in the Indian subcontinent, apart from thousands of thakurs, talukdars, zamindaris, and jagirs. Princely states covered 40% of the area of pre-independent India and constituted 23% of its population.

Mahatma Gandhi became a leader of the Indian community and over the years developed a political movement based on the methods of non-violent civil disobedience, which he called "satyagraha". Mahatma Gandhi (October 2, 1869 to January 30, 1948) was the leader of India's non-violent independence movement against British rule and in South Africa. He advocated for the civil rights of Indians. He was killed by a fanatic, one of his own followers, in 1948.

Chapter 17 – Oregon 2020

Conifer/Neem

"Not every dream grows on every land, so you got to watch out! "Sugar cane" dreams should find the environment where there is flooding of great ideas from great people. It will die off if it is planted at the place where the drought of discouragement is a well cherished culture!"
— Israelmore Ayivor, *The Great Hand Book of Quotes*

Summer was almost to an end and Conifer was out in his favorite place inventorying his crop yields on a spreadsheet. He believed his garden had grown a plentiful harvest, but Conifer had no previous gardens to compare his numbers with and the only data he could find came from different locations, with contrasting temperatures, soil content and rainfall amounts. The constants were too variable to make an accurate point of reference. This summer, he had accumulated fifty-seven carrots, forty-five bunches of lettuce leaves, eighty-three ears of corn, ninety-nine pea pods, thirty-two tomatoes, twenty-four cucumbers, seventeen squash gourds, and nine pumpkins. His mound growing crops could use a few more weeks of warm weather. Next year perhaps he would begin their seeds inside like he had the tomato plants to create a longer growing season. He would miss his garden over the long winter months, but he could use that time to plan new strategies for spring planting.

His mother raved over his garden produce both in size and plentiful outcome, but the three of them were having trouble consuming all the fresh vegetables he had produced. Brooke Ridgeway had begun sharing them with their neighbors and friends. Maybe next year Conifer would build a vegetable stand along the road with a sign that listed all the prices. That way he would only have to use minimal communication by gestures with any customers who stopped by. Conifer had never considered farming as a career, but it was honest, worthwhile work and would be a valuable skill. People always needed food.

Juniper burst into Conifer's quiet growing space accompanied by her rescue friend and rescued beast. All three were heading his way. "Hey Conifer, would you like to go driving with Stetson and me? You can come and see how good I'm getting and if you want to, you could spend some time behind the wheel too."

Conifer wondered if his sister was preparing to become a professional driver of some kind with all of the hours that she had logged practicing driving with Stetson…possibly a taxi, uber or lift driver, maybe a limousine chauffer or even race car driver? Conifer had already gone with them a couple of times and would much rather stay right where he was watching his vegetables grow. The communication between his sister and guy friend was exhausting with too many references where Conifer had absolutely no idea what they really meant. But even an autistic person could pick up on the fact that they liked each other and that he was the third wheel, or actually more like the fifth wheel, in the car.

Conifer politely declined the offer with the rhythmic reply, "*And if she should tell you come closer, and if she tempts you with her charms, tell her no no no no no-no-no-no, no no no no no-no-no-no, no no no no no, Tell Her No.*"

"One '*no*' would have been plenty Conifer, but I get the message," Juniper replied somewhere between entertained and annoyed by his answer, Conifer could not really tell which one. "If you would rather stay here anyway, since it is such a nice day, can I leave Dr. Strange out back with you?"

The real Dr. Strange was Conifer's favorite superhero and the most powerful sorcerer in the world. Dr. Strange had the ability to tap into mystical energy invoked by spells, incantations or by the power of divine beings. This power helped him to manipulate the forces of the universe. The real Dr. was a good superhero to have around and Juniper's dog bearing the same name was not nearly as annoying as Conifer had feared he might be. Conifer didn't make as much mental effort as usual to find the perfect song to respond to his sister's question, but this one by Rihanna would work.

"Not really sure how to feel about it, something in the way you move makes me feel like I can't live without you… I want you to stay." Conifer completed his lyrics looking down at the dog so Juniper would know the words were intended for Dr. Strange and not for her or Stetson. They could go off and have their drive.

"I didn't know you felt so strongly about the little guy, but thanks bunches Conifer. I owe you." His sister said as she and her driving instructor bounded through the fence gate towards their get-away vehicle. The dog followed them part of the way across the lawn and then distracted by some smell wandered off to roam on his own. Babysitting a dog in a fenced backyard was not difficult. Conifer would make sure to pet the pooch a few times to fulfill his assignment properly.

A thought flowing from newly arrived Neem poured into Conifer's head. Neem did not usually show up when others were around or if he was there Conifer could not hear him as easily. "Your crop is impressive Conifer. You have done a wonderful job with the garden."

"Do you have a garden, or have you ever grown one?" Conifer was curious.

"I guess you could call it that, sort of, but what we grew was over a much bigger area with less variety of plants. I am from a family of farmers, so we planted and harvested very large gardens for many years," Neem responded.

"Then you will be a good resource for advice," Conifer felt almost enthusiastic.

"Your gardening skills and implements may have already surpassed my own," Neem admitted. "And having access to water from rubber hosing is life-changing. You must never experience drought."

"Different parts of the world do experience extreme dryness and drought conditions, but Oregon is a pretty wet area geographically, especially the western side of the state," Conifer shared. "Fertilizer helps the growth too."

"Have you determined your science fair idea or come up with any angle for your project yet?" Neem prompted.

"There are so many things to choose from, maybe testing the effectiveness of different fertilizers?" Conifer brainstormed.

"That could be valuable knowledge to research, but it might take a few growing seasons to perfect the results. What about preventing drought? You could possibly find a way to fill clouds with water. Maybe stimulating clouds to attract moisture and then directly release it where needed? Possibly gather moisture from oceans if there is not enough in area lakes and then redistribute it." Neem pondered mentally sharing.

"I believe that technology already exists," Conifer informed his friend. "Ski resorts use weather modification to create snow by cloud seeding. It is an enhancement of nature that forms ice crystals by seeding the atmosphere with chemicals such as silver iodide or dry ice. They work to promote rainfall by inducing nucleation. The water that is present in the air condenses around the newly introduced particles and crystallizes to form ice."

"You have so much knowledge in that brain of yours, Conifer. Is this technology used for farmers too?" Neem asked.

"I don't think so," Conifer puzzled in his head. "Cloud-seeders can't make rain appear out of the clear blue sky. Rather, they create snow and sometimes rain where it's most likely to occur from clouds. Clouds are already full of water vapor, but sometimes the water needs to be coaxed into forming the ice crystals needed for snow. I am not sure how they would be able to create snow or rain without clouds."

"That is the problem then. Most drought areas I have been familiar with have pretty clear skies with not a cloud in sight. What if your project was to create artificial clouds and then use the cloud seeding technology to deliver water to wherever it is needed in the world?"

"That would be a magic trick for sure. We might need Dr. Stranger's superpowers to help manipulate the forces of the universe for that one," Conifer mentally interjected.

"How do we contact this Dr. Strange?" Neem asked excitedly.

"The fake one is over there digging a hole in the grass," Conifer directed.

"Do you mean the dog?" Conifer could feel Neem's confusion.

"I think I just made my very first joke, but perhaps it wasn't very funny." Conifer hoped Neem could sense he was smiling. "Dr. Strange is the dog's name, and I am not even sure the original Dr. Strange is a real character, but we will need to use the same skills that he possesses, including manipulation of the powers of the universe, to make this project work."

"You are a clever young man Conifer and with both of us working together – or even all three of us - perhaps we can come up with something that just might work." Neem's positive energy force flowed between them. "One never knows what can happen when two minds from two different realms come together and access the knowledge of the universe."

Conifer's mind was slightly blown with that comment. He knew there was more inside of his brain than what he was able to use as fully as he would like to. Maybe with Neem's influence they could access all they needed for this project idea. "I am willing to work on imagining and hopefully creating a potential formula."

"We won't know if we can do it unless we try." Neem responded before he seemed to withdraw as quickly as he had come. Conifer never knew when to expect his visits or how long they would last, but each one was meaningful to him.

As if the dog could read Conifer's mind too, Dr. Strange wandered over to where Conifer sat on the deck steps considering Neem's words and plopped himself down on Conifer's vacant lap. Usually, touch of any kind was uncomfortable for Conifer, but the dog's presence did not seem to agitate him. Perhaps the little guy did possess some of his namesake's magical superpowers. Conifer redirected his thoughts towards the dog.

"Well hairy canine, would you like to make it a trio and help Neem and I save the world from drought?" Conifer knew how crazy the thought sounded even to himself, but all great inventors and likely even sorcerers had to begin somewhere.

Chapter 17 notes: Children and adults with autism spectrum disorder often care deeply but lack the ability to spontaneously develop empathic and socially connected typical behavior. They want to socially interact but do not know how. If one identical twin has autism spectrum disorder, there is a 60-96% chance the other twin will have some form of ASD. Although with fraternal twins the percentage of both having ASD decreases to a 24% chance. Each child with autism spectrum disorder is a unique individual; people with ASD differ as much from one another as do all people. Autism spectrum disorder costs a family $60,000 a year on average.

Cloud seeding is a real science. Chemicals such as silver iodide or dry ice are induced into clouds inducing nucleation which promotes snow or rainfall. Water in the air condenses around the newly introduced particles and crystallizes to form ice. However, the science of creating clouds to be used for the seeding has not been discovered- yet.

Conifer's song lyrics - *Tell Her No* by The Zombies and *Stay* by Rihanna.

Chapter 18 – Oregon 2020

Brooke

"The world is a drought when out of love." - Brandon Boyd

Brooke watched through the window as her son sort of snuggled an actual live dog in his lap, well maybe the dog was doing more of the snuggling, but it was still an unlikely scenario to behold. The fact that Conifer had not immediately flung the dog off onto the ground was impressive. Maybe Juniper had been right about the puppy, Dr. Strange had definite service dog potential. Brooke knew she could not protect Conifer from every uncomfortable encounter that came his way and it appeared he was able to handle more than she gave him credit for. She mentally captured the postcard moment displayed before her to pull out again later when she needed it during more difficult mom-times.

How had she arrived at this place in her life? If anyone had told her as a budding dancer and thespian in high school that she would become a suburban, stay-at-home mom with a couple of kids in less than ten years she would never have believed them. She even had the fenced yard, maybe not an iconic white picket fence but close enough, and a garden that grew their own vegetables. The strangest part was that even though in her wildest dreams (or nightmares) she could never have imagined her present existence; she wouldn't choose anything different now. Her children were her world and at times she felt the only role she lived to fulfill was that of a mother.

Juniper was bright, tough, feisty and courageous. Mother and daughter relationships were complicated, but the two of them were friends or at least friendly most of the time. Junie did not look a thing like Brooke and was stronger than her mother in many ways. Brooke understood that life with a brother who had autism could not be easy, but Juniper was not one to complain. Brooke leaned on her daughter as a support system more than she liked to admit. Juniper was becoming a solid nearly-adult and was going to be okay. The girl had found her own place and way in the world.

Conifer looked more like his mother, but that is where the similarity ended. Imagining Conifer with any desire to perform on stage like she had was ridiculously impossible. Brooke wasn't able to decipher what her son experienced in his private world, but she wanted to keep him safe in hers. She sensed that the boy had brilliance encapsulated inside that brain of his. Just the amount of song lyrics that he held cataloged had to take up major space, then the fact that he had figured out such a creative way to communicate with those lyrics took computer-like brainpower. On top of that was the infinite scientific knowledge he stored in that head of his. Brooke hoped and had to believe that one day he would be able to access and share it more easily with others. Conifer was still finding himself and figuring it all out. Boys matured a little later than girls.

The teenage duo only had a couple more years before they would be off on their own, well Juniper would, Brooke wasn't sure what would happen with Conifer. Or what would happen with herself at that point for that matter? Brooke knew that Blaze expected her to return to New York after the twins graduated. Blaze had no plans to ever move to Oregon and if she was honest with herself, she did not plan to move back to NYC unless the kids went to college there. Brooke was past her prime for stage work and she had no desire to play the socialite wife again. The years had sped by and she and Blaze had grown constantly further apart instead of growing closer. Though she had never looked elsewhere for male companionship, she was engaging and friendly so a few men in Oregon knowing she lived alone had gotten the wrong signals, but nothing had become of it. She had no time for an extramarital relationship, her own was confusing enough.

Her parents, Emily and Darren Fountain, had made marriage look so easy. According to them, a couple merely found one another, fell in love, got married and made it work. They had lived their whole lives in the same small Midwestern town where they raised Brooke and her brother to work hard and follow their own dreams. However, neither of their children's dreams had kept them in Missouri. Her brother enlisted in the air force upon high school graduation. The military paid Tim's way through college and he retired at the rank of lieutenant colonel after a full career stationed all over the world with deployments to places where no one wanted to live. Tim now flew part-time as a pilot for American Airlines out of their Dallas/Ft. Worth hub. He lived much closer to their parents than Brooke did, and his family visited Missouri more frequently, not only due to their geographic location but also their flight benefits and their kids who did not have any environmental issues.

Brooke could have been a more attentive daughter, but she had been too busy trying to make it as a Broadway dancer, then as a wife, and then as a mother of twins, one of which had special needs. She had her excuses all lined up and even though her parent's retirement pension didn't enable them to travel much, they still could have found a way to come and visit her more often. They were content with their lives and with each other and they called Brooke once a week to check in on her family and offer encouragement. They had been nothing but encouraging her whole life, so why did she feel neglected now?

Wrapping up her pity party, Brooke looked at the time and realized that she needed to leave for Conifer's school. Principal Martinelli had requested a meeting with her at two o'clock and she felt a little nervous as to what it might be about. Juniper wasn't back from her driving lesson yet, but Conifer was old enough to be left alone, so Brooke hollered out the backdoor that she had a meeting at his school and would be back in about an hour or so. She was not really sure how long the appointment would take, but she could not imagine that the principal had all afternoon to shoot the breeze with her since school was starting next week.

On the drive over to the school Brooke thought through every scenario that as an adult she could possibly be called into the principal's office for. She was not sure any of her guesses made sense. Conifer was not a model student, but he was definitely not a problem one. He got excellent grades, was not disruptive and the school year hadn't even started yet. Perhaps it was more about class placement or changes in his

IEP (Individual Education Plan), but Brooke usually dealt directly with Conifer's teachers for those. She liked Mr. Martinelli and knew that he was very involved with his students, so she tried not to stress about the meeting.

Oak Leaf Academy's secretary showed Brooke into the principal's office and pointed to a chair across from his desk motioning for her to take a seat.

"Welcome Mrs. Ridgeway, thank you for coming, Mr. Martinelli will be with you shortly," and she was out the door before finishing her sentence.

Either the woman was ultra-efficient or a tad on the spectrum herself Brooke noted. She looked around the room while she waited. The principal had created a welcoming spot for his special student group. The décor was not so busy that it would overstimulate anyone with autism, but cozy enough not to feel like a prison cell either for those who were not. The ice blue walls displayed a few pictures of past student groupings. A tidy bookshelf covered the wall to the right of the large oak desk and a short navy sofa was pressed up against the opposite wall on the left. The door and a wall of glazed glass blocks, that let in light but not nosy sightseers, was directly behind Brooke. The combination was sleek yet manly. She wondered if there was a Mrs. Martinelli who helped with the decorating or if Principal Martinelli just had instinctive good taste.

"Mrs. Ridgeway, so sorry to keep you waiting, there is always more that needs to be done before the first day of school than I remember each year." The tall, slender man sat down gracefully behind the desk looking steadily into Brooke's eyes. He had a gentle manner about him and definitely did not seem to be anywhere on the spectrum.

"Please call me, Brooke," Brooke offered. "And how would you prefer I addressed you?"

"The students call me Mr. M.," he said pointing downward with his first three fingers, "but Chad would be just fine," Mr. M. or Chad replied. Brooke didn't think Mr. Martinelli seemed at all like a Chad, more an Alexander maybe. Conifer's principal appeared to be between Blaze and her own age, the man carried his sharply dressed exterior quite well and exuded a calming strength. She would be more comfortable calling him Mr. Martinelli or Mr. M., but it was too late now. "Thank you for taking the time to meet with me today," He smiled.

Brooke wanted to get right to the point and find out why her presence had been requested, but she wondered if being that direct would be rude, so the two carried on small-talk conversation getting to know one another for a few minutes before Mr. M. circled in on the subject of her summons.

"Brooke, I am aware that you spent some time working on Broadway before you moved here," Mr. Martinelli stated. "Tell me a little about that."

"I am not sure what you would like to know. I did work on Broadway for a few years, never as a lead or star in a performance or anything like that. I was in the ensemble cast of a few big shows before the twins were born. Conifer has a twin sister at Bend High School in case you didn't know," Brooke shared. Perhaps Principal Martinelli wanted her to hook him up with Broadway tickets, but she really didn't have any connections there anymore.

"I think the information about Conifer's sister is in his file, but today I am more interested in your background. Do you sing, dance, or direct? What is your theatrical experience, Brooke?" Chad's eyes held steady on her face not missing a thing.

"I guess I have done pretty much everything in the realm of theater, besides directing a show, but I have been exposed to directors enough that I probably have amateur directing skills too. Why do you ask?" Brooke was getting slightly uncomfortable and ready for Principal Martinelli to spit out whatever he wanted. No more beating around the metaphorical bush.

"Well, in short, I attended an educational conference over the summer where we discussed some outstanding new ideas on how best to bring out the most in our special group of students. I learned that some schools have had great success in doing a schoolwide musical each year. It does not have to be of professional quality, of course, I am not expecting that, so I believe you are more than qualified for our needs. Theater would not be one of the regular classes in their curriculum, but an after school elective opportunity for any interested students. Music connects us all on a different level." Principal Chad paused to get her reaction.

"What would this position entail for me? Or what exactly would you want me to do?" Brooke asked.

"Pretty much everything concerning or having to do with the performance. You would have full access to the school's facilities and full support of our staff. You could select any musical that is appropriate for our crowd. I feel you will be especially aware of the parameters having a son in your own home as a resource. I would expect you to audition and cast the students in fitting roles, choreograph the scenes and dance numbers, teach the songs and direct the overall play. I realize it sounds like a lot, but there are a few members of the staff who have already volunteered to help out. Or if you prefer, you can select your own assistants to work with. What do you think?" Mr. M. asked hopefully. "Can we count on you?"

"I am not sure what to think, you caught me totally off guard," Brooke had not even been in the ballpark with any of her what-the-principal-wanted guesses, "And I also think it sounds a little overwhelming, but I do love the theater and I think it might be a meaningful opportunity. Can I give you a tentative yes and consider my options overnight?"

"Of course, I am thrilled that you will even consider putting together a show for us. I know you haven't said yes yet, but I have a good feeling about us working together. I will wait to hear back from you tomorrow." And with that Mr. M. stood up signaling it was time for Brooke's exit.

On Brooke's drive home thoughts of a different variety than those on the drive to the school flooded her head. What was she thinking? Was it even possible to do a musical with autistic kids…or kids with autism? Then her questions of doubt were replaced by ideas of possible musicals that Conifer's school could perform. *Newsies* and *Dear Evan Hansen* would be entertaining musicals that lent themselves to a teenage cast, but she reasoned, *Newsies* might have too much dancing to pull off. And the subject matter of *Dear Evan*

Hansen might be too heavy and deep for the cast's demographic. She didn't want to cause the students to overly focus on suicide. *Les Mis* and *Hamilton* were both awesome shows with all the dialog done in musical lyrics and many of *Hamilton's* songs were written using the rap-style singing which Conifer was proficient at, but these shows had too much production value to attempt as a first-time director. A Disney show might be Oak Leaf friendly, and there were so many to choose from - *The Lion King, Aladdin* or *Mary Poppins* might be fun. Brooke hadn't even agreed to do a show yet and here she was brainstorming shows, reign it in girl.

Then an inspiration hit her, *Matilda* would be the perfect show to do. It was a quirky play anyway and many scenes took place in a school. The musical should be easier for her very literal cast members to relate to. She pictured a few simple set design ideas with snippets of choreography dancing through them in her mind. Okay, maybe she really was going to do this. Brooke was starting to feel the energy and get the buzz in her gut that came when she performed theater on stage. She would take into consideration Conifer's input before making her final decision, but it would be good to be more involved in his school life. She might learn a few things there that would help her relate better to him at home. She would not agree to do the show unless Conifer was willing to participate. He could be in the ensemble cast; Brooke knew firsthand there was nothing wrong with that. Or be cast in a small principle role with just a few lines - what was the name of that boy who had to eat the whole cake? Conifer could surely rap a few lines from the script, heck he may already have them stored in his brain, or he could memorize and regurgitate a few spoken lines as he did with all of his scientific data.

Brooke could hardly wait to get home and share her big news with the family. What a difference only an hour could make in a person's view of the world. Enthusiasm and excitement had replaced the neglected feeling in her heart. She wondered if Juniper might consider being her assistant director for the musical, it would be a wonderful experience working together and making it a family affair. That is if her dog-loving-daughter could sever her attachment to the Rescue for a few months. Or was Juniper's attachment more to a certain male of her own species that worked there with her, the googly-eyed guy that had been driving Juniper around a lot lately?

It looked like Stetson's Impala was parked in front of the house, so Juniper was back home along with her self-appointed driving instructor. The Ridgeways had a few things they would need to figure out before *Matilda* could begin coming to life on Oak Leaf Academy's stage, but with any luck, Brooke might be turning the first page of a script opening a new adventure for them all.

Chapter 18 notes: A study by Olivia Clement published in the Journal of Autism and Developmental Disorders (October 2015) found that theatre may help improve social competence for children with autism spectrum disorder. The study brings to light recent discussions and efforts in the theatre community in making theatre more accessible to people with ASD.

Chapter 19 – Oregon 2020

Juniper

"If it wasn't for rain, the world would be a barren & dry place. Much like a heart without love &happiness." — *Anthony T. Hincks*

Juniper sat down on their couch next to Stetson having just completed their most recent driving/kissing double lesson. He had followed her into the house, and she was trying to decide if she should invite him to stay for dinner. They sat close to touching, but not quite pressed together, and she could feel the heat radiating between their two bodies. Juniper was becoming a competent driver and felt prepared to take her driving test, but she was not sure how she was doing in the kissing category. She wondered if that was the main reason Stetson took her driving in the first place - not to help her improve at driving, but for the make-out sessions. Was she paying her instructor with kisses from her slightly swollen lips? When school started next week would she remain a behind the scenes, secret pastime in Stetson's life or would he actually acknowledge her presence in the Bend High hallways? It was a dilemma that would soon be sorted out.

It was entertaining to watch her car-time beau trying to have a conversation with her most stoic brother. Stetson was doing quite well in picking up on Conifer's pop song lyric replies. She had to give the guy an A-plus for effort at least. She liked Stetson more than she wanted to admit and he seemed to return the emotional connection, but Juniper's no-so-vast experience with the opposite sex was derived mainly from movies and books, so he could be toying with her affections for all she knew.

Even more shocking than the in-progress Conifer/Stetson conversation was witnessing Dr. Strange follow Conifer into the house and lay down at his feet even after she tried to call the puppy over. Did her brother have a bone in his pocket or was he harboring some dog whisperer skills that Juniper was heretofore unaware of? Maybe the boy and beast were becoming a superhero duo combining their own unique otherworldly powers. It had been an interesting day and there were still several hours yet to go.

Brooke burst through the front door with more enthusiasm than Juniper had seen in her mother since…well, since forever. "I am glad you are all here," her mom said before she came to a complete stop, but her quick glance at Stetson left his presence in the questionable category. "My meeting with Principal Martinelli was interesting…a total surprise…and there is something I need to ask you two about."

Stetson had enough social awareness to realize that there were three other people in the room so he asked, "Would you like me to leave Mrs. Ridgeway?"

"I suppose it is okay if you stay, Stetson. What I have to say is not a secret and perhaps you can lend your support in some way," Juniper's mom became a bit more thoughtful. Maybe Brooke was realizing how helpful Stetson had been lately and her mother didn't even know about the extra two-for-one, the double-lesson deal he was giving her daughter.

"Conifer, your principal asked me to direct a musical for your school. But first, I need to make sure that you are okay with it, and then Juniper, I was hoping you might be willing to help as an assistant director … if you are interested or have the time?" Brooke poured out her combined questions in one big breath.

So many thoughts were instantly ricocheting around in Juniper's head. The play would definitely have to be a comedy or at least a comedy of errors with its unique cast. Maybe it would be more of a tragedy, it was hard to imagine which way the production would go. But since her mother seemed to have sucked in more life than she had seen Brooke possess for the past few years, what came out of Juniper's mouth was, "Sure mom, I will help you when I can, working around my hours at the rescue, if the practices are after school, and if Conifer is okay with the idea."

Although theater had been the center of her mother's pre-children world, Juniper knew virtually nothing about it besides what she had gleaned from an observer's standpoint. This opportunity seemed to be uber-important to her mom, so Juniper did not want to be the killjoy in the equation. She gave her positive response before Conifer had time to come up with his lyrical reply.

Conifer still seemed to be juggling his answer, so Stetson interjected his thoughts. "I'm not really comfortable with performing and not a part of the student body, so being in the show is probably not something you would want me to do anyway. I am pretty handy with a hammer and saw if you need my amateur carpentry skills to help build the sets or anything." Stetson volunteered.

"Thank you, that is very generous, but I guess we need to find out what Conifer feels about this possibility before we go any further. I know it might be overwhelming, but are you

171

willing to let me try?" Her mother asked her son with a touch of pleading in her voice.

"*Baby, there's an enormous crowd of people. They're all after my blood. I wish maybe they'd tear down the walls of this theater. Let me out, let me out,*" Conifer began. It had taken him a while to find this obscure lyric. Juniper thought it sounded like an old rock song from before their time and it did not sound like Conifer was comfortable with the show at all. But just when they all thought it was a definite no-go, her brother continued the monotone melody from the same song.

"*But I must let the show go, I must let the show go, I must let the show go on.*" Conifer finished.

The rest of the room digested Conifer's lyric-comments and her mother asked the question they all were wondering, "Let me see if I understand correctly. You don't really want to be a part of the show, but you are willing to let me direct it for the school?"

Conifer nodded his head and added, "*Wish I could be part of that world.*"

Juniper did recognize the source of this lyric; Conifer was clever enough to use a line from another musical. "By the way mom, what musical did you plan to do? Sounds like Conifer is putting in a bid for *The Little Mermaid*."

"I think the sets for *The Little Mermaid* might be too difficult to create, I thought of maybe doing *Matilda*. However, I only want to commit such a large amount of time volunteering at Conifer's school if he wants to be a part of the performance too." Her mom sounded disappointed.

Conifer began shaking his head back and forth while repeating, *"I must let the show go, I must let the show go, I must let the show go on."*

"Okay Conifer, it is okay," her mom soothed. "We can put together a show for your school. I bet we can find a small part in the production for you or even some job backstage that you would be comfortable working on. What do you think?" Brooke continued to calm her son while attempting to understand him at the same time.

Conifer shrugged his shoulders but did not endeavor to clarify his response with any more lyrics. It looked like their mom was going to leave it there for now.

Stetson interrupted the silence, "sounds like you will be pushing a major load uphill trying to pull off a play at Oak Academy. The kids in theater at Bend High say the plays at our school are even intense to put together. Why do you think the principal asked you to put together a musical for the whole school Mrs. Ridgeway?"

173

"Mr. Martinelli said researchers have seen positive results from introducing theater into the autistic spectrum community. It is impressive he wants to give it a try." Brooke responded omitting her personal experience in the arena.

"And my mom was a big deal on Broadway before we came along," Juniper added.

"Not a big deal, but I did dance in the ensemble cast of some pretty big shows," Brooke admitted. "Organizing a full musical is still a stretch for me, but I think it is a positive goal and I am honored to be asked to try to accomplish it."

"I am impressed. Count me in Mrs. Ridgeway." Stetson reinforced his offer.

"And I know much less than you do about most things, mom, but especially about theater. If you still want me to help, I will be happy to do whatever I can." Juniper added.

Conifer added nothing else verbally. He did not seem agitated anymore as he sat back down and began stroking the dog at his feet. It appeared Dr. Strange did have a soothing effect on her brother.

"Mom, can Stetson stay for dinner since you are going to put him to work - food for his wages?" Juniper asked out loud before realizing that she should have asked her mother in private first.

But before her mother could respond, Stetson replied, "Thanks for the offer, but I have to get to my shift at the dog rescue soon. You know the place where 'all dogs go to heaven, but hopefully just not yet'," he grinned using the lengthy name of the rescue where they both worked. "Unfortunately, not all of the dogs there have found homes as great as Dr. Strange has so someone has to tend to them." Stetson reached down and patted the dog at Conifer's feet before beginning to leave.

There was no goodbye kiss in front of the family as Stetson exited through the Ridgeway's front door, but he did turn and toss a glimmer of hope her way. "Hey Juni-per, I was just thinking, you must have inherited some pretty amazing dance moves with your mom being a Broadway dancer and all. How about going to a dance with me after school starts? I know there is a Homecoming one that will be coming up before long."

Juniper was not so sure about any hidden dance moves that she may possess, but she was thrilled that she was not going to remain merely a car-kissing secret at high school this year. "That sounds like so much fun Stetson. I will see what I can come up with. Maybe we can rip-off some of Michael Jackson's moves and workup part of his *Thriller* music video to stun the Bend High crowd with, some of the other students may even want to join in."

175

Conifer unexpectedly jumped onto his feet and into their parting conversation pretending to be a zombie he spoke-sang in his monotone way, "'*Cause this is thriller, thriller night and no one's gonna save you from the beast about to strike. You know it's thriller, thriller night...*'"

Juniper and Stetson listened to Conifer rap a few more lines and then looked at each other and laughed, not at Conifer, but in the spontaneous joy of the moment.

Stetson turned back to Conifer still chuckling and offered, "With those skills, it looks like you could pull off any part in your mother's play Conifer. Or at least let Juniper and I dig you up a date, so you can double with us to the Bend High dance. You are one musical dude, man."

The horror that flashed across Conifer's face was far more terrifying than his *Thriller* song impression. Juniper was pretty sure that she and Stetson would be going as a solo couple to any dance that they did happen to attend together this school year.

Chapter 19 notes: Conifer's song lyrics- *The Show Must Go On* by Three Dog Night, *A Whole New World* by Jodi Benson, and *Thriller* by Michael Jackson

Chapter 20 – Paradise 1948

Anoop

"Friends are 'annuals' that need seasonal nurturing to bear blossoms. Family is a 'perennial' that comes up year after year, enduring the droughts of absence and neglect. There's a place in the garden for both of them."
- Erma Bombeck

Anoop was still reveling in being together with his big brother again as the two of them traveled seamlessly into another realm. Reyansh had not spoken a word to him but Anoop knew everything his brother was thinking and feeling. Their communication was streamlined - mind to mind and heart to heart. Anoop felt wrapped in a blanket of warmth and love. In fact, the best word he could come up with to describe his new environment was *love*. Everything around him oozed love. The manifestation of love was tangible here.

The other adjective Anoop would use was *light*. Colors were more vibrant and alive. Every object surrounding him was painted with light and illuminated beyond its very essence. His brother Reyansh had become a being of light. For all of these years, Anoop had worried about what his brother missed out on by leaving earth so early. He now realized how misplaced and wasted his worry had been. Anoop's new address was unknown, but this location was far better than anything he had imagined when pondering his next life during his previous one.

Was he waiting to be reincarnated or was this his mother's heaven? Wherever he was, Anoop realized he shouldn't have spent a minute worrying about his brother. Anoop clung to earth-life with tenacity, not knowing the amazing world that next awaited him. The clinging was probably for the best, a person needed to appreciate every minute of wherever they were and magnify their time there. Knowing how wonderful what lay beyond was going to be, would have been a distraction. Anoop's greatest surprise was that he was not really dead but still himself. He had brought the best of what made him himself with him. There may be less physical substance to him, but whatever he was, was wonderful. He could move and reason with ease beyond his previous capacity.

Anoop turned to Reyansh and forgetting that he didn't need to speak out loud asked, "Are we in heaven?"

178

His brother's reply filled all of Anoop, "Where we now dwell has many names on earth...the Afterlife, Nirvana, Moksha... we are in Paradise. One of the transitory places where we wait for our final placement."

"But you have been here for so long, why are you still waiting?" Anoop wordlessly asked.

"Time is not measured here as you know it, Anoop. There is no beginning and no end to time. We live forever and we have always been. It may take a while to internalize the magnitude of who you are." Anoop's knowledgeable guide informed him.

"What have you been doing all this time?" As Anoop wondered this, Reyansh perceived his thoughts.

"We keep very busy. We are still learning and growing, minds have great capacity and only a very small portion of their power is accessed on earth. Our greatest assignment is to watch over and assist those still sojourning on their earthly path." Reyansh explained. "Did you ever feel my presence near you back on the farm near Agra? I was often there."

"I'm not sure. Perhaps that is why I was drawn to go and speak to you, or to your gravesite and those of our sisters, nearly every day." Anoop remembered.

"Would you like to see our sisters?" Reyansh asked?

"They are all here too?" Anoop could barely contain his enthusiasm and felt like running or flying or floating or whatever the mode of transportation was up here to meet them. "Yes, yes, please," he replied.

Moments after wishing to see his sisters, Anoop stood amidst them…Viti Hope, Pia Grace, Devya Joy and Zahira Faith. He did not know which was which, but he remembered all of their names from those etched into the wooden crosses back home. But now this was his home, everything was happening so fast and was all so mind-blowingly impossible. If his brother had appeared dazzling to him, his sisters were absolutely magnificent. They were no longer the little girls that he remembered but beautiful young women displaying features from both of his parents in various combinations. Powerful emotions welled up in Anoop's breast and spilled onto his face, this place truly was paradise.

The six siblings gathered in a heavenly family reunion, a reception to welcome Anoop to this new realm. Anoop was not aware how long they interacted because time was not measured here, thus everything was timeless, but he could have basked in their company forever catching up on all of the brother/sister moments he had missed. An apology for not being able to achieve something outstanding in their honor poured from Anoop's heart and soul. Complete and total absolution was returned from the five that surrounded him and one of his sisters comforted him with the knowledge, "Dear brother, do you not understand that you did well on earth…the most important acts are to love those around you. Understand that you will be able to accomplish much more from our perspective here and that you have all of eternity to fulfill your goal."

The truth of her words wafted over him and Anoop felt a satisfying calmness. After an undetermined number of minutes, others Anoop had known, who had long since departed the same physical world he had recently left behind, stopped by to welcome him as well. When finally introduced to his Sharma grandparents, his baba's parents expressed deep pain for their intolerant actions. His repentant ancestors acknowledged that they had made restitution for their appalling behavior towards him. Anoop felt no animosity, just joy in the connection they could now savor. Even Dada John Fountain was there. The true hero of many stories from Anoop's youth stood before him in all of his glory. This grandpa's light seemed a bit brighter than the rest. Perhaps the man earned a head start by gathering light from the former life of sacrifice that he had lived. Anoop was pleased he would have plenty of time to get to know all of his grandparents and great grandparents whom he had been denied time with on earth. Family relationships were the true treasures of paradise.

Memories of his days on earth and his previous life there were still present, but the pain of leaving was gone. Anoop knew with every fiber of his being that Padma and his other children would be okay, whatever happened, until they joined him here.

There were three more people Anoop longed to see and as thoughts of his ma and baba filled his mind, he could see the two of them in the distance as they began walking towards him. His ma looked much the same, but the lines of hard living had been erased from her lovely face, and she was even more radiant than Anoop remembered. Baba Mehul was not at all the same as the day he left earth, old age had dropped away and he was once again a youthful man similar in age to his beloved Hiya. The intense love they possessed for one another was tangible and encompassed Anoop as well.

Between his parents, holding one hand of each, walked an almost iridescent young woman. The girl had a familiar look about her, but Anoop was not sure who she was - perhaps a cousin or maybe another sibling?

As the trio drew nearer his ma smiled and spoke, "Son meet your daughter, Aashi."

Could this delightful girl be the infant that he and Padma had lost so many years ago? Had she been here all this time in the keeping and care of his own ma? Tears composed of some purified substance drizzled down Anoop's cheeks as he took this daughter into his arms. Hugs were less fleshy in this dimension, but the sentiment was the same and a warmth burned in his heart.

"Papa, I have watched you and loved you while waiting until you arrived." Aashi's mental voice was tinkling and sweet. "Grandmother and the aunties have been ever so gracious and loving to me, but it gave me a deeper identity to know who I was and where I came from on earth. I have loved you and my ma, and Briary Padma, Reyansh, and Noopi from afar."

Anoop had never experienced the depth and immensity of feelings that swirled inside his perfected self. He wished his Padma could be here to meet their incredible daughter, but he knew Padma would join them at her designated time when her destined journey was complete and that her arrival would be in virtually no time from paradise's reckoning.

Anoop wondered what Aashi had witnessed of their lives on the farm. Had his daughter been proud of her heritage or seen things that gave her sadness and concern? "You were loved and missed every day on earth dear Aashi. Can we look down right now and see how everyone is doing back there?" Anoop asked.

"All in good time beta, but wouldn't you rather explore your new home first?" His father asked.

"When I see with my own eyes that everyone who I left behind is okay, paradise will be even more a place of peace for me," Anoop admitted.

"Very well," and as his baba said these words the four of them stood in front of a portal-like screen which displayed a panoramic view of what was happening in the home Anoop had left. He saw his body lying completely still on the bed. Padma, his wife, a woman of very little emotion was visibly distressed and Briary Padma, his other daughter, was openly weeping at his bedside. Noopi was speaking with the grandchildren telling them how Dada Anoop had gone to a better place and they mustn't be sad because he was happy.

Anoop did feel happiness, but he would be happier if his death was not making the rest of his family so sad. "How can I let them know I am near? I want them to know I am just fine and will be watching over them." Anoop felt a bit frantic from his lack of ability to comfort them.

"After some practice, you will be able to comfort those in the other dimension and even communicate

184

proficiently with those who are in tune to things of a spiritual nature," his father informed him.

"How will that work?" Anoop asked.

"Travel is extremely efficient in your spirit form and the abilities of the mind are endless." Anoop's mother explained. "I was with your family on several special occasions after I passed away. Oh, Anoop and I have met my mother Isolde here in paradise. She shared with me that she was near me during my hardest times on earth. I wish I had known."

"And I went with Grandma Briary on her visits sometimes." Aashi added. "I was with her to guide Grandpa Mehul here when he left earth and for a few more festive times too."

"We can do more from here than is possible with our limited abilities below. I would have been an amazing farmer with all the knowledge I now possess." Mehul lamented.

"Even through all the droughts?" Anoop was skeptical.

"Weather always presents a challenge, but the dry conditions would not have been as devastating for sure." Mehul admitted. "And all of the lives that were lost are not seen as such a great tragedy from this perspective. They merely arrived in paradise sooner."

Anoop marveled at the difference in understanding a few hours can make.

"Why don't you stay with us beta, at least until you get your bearings up here and decide where you want to serve." Mehul offered.

"Yes, that would be wonderful, you can retrieve some time lost with Aashi on earth and get to know your celestial daughter better." Briary added hopefully.

For the first time Anoop really understood that his desire to do something great had not died with him. He still had the opportunity to help his fellow man and leave a mark on an earth he no longer dwelt upon. There were millions of beings that could benefit from the enlightened understanding and enhanced knowledge he could glean and share from his elevated perspective. Brother Reyansh had explained to him that there were vast places of information in Paradise that he could have access if interested. Anoop was relieved that he had already learned to read so he could jump right into studying any subject he chose. He needed to determine where to focus his altruistic energies first. Instead of honoring his siblings who had passed on like he had preciously hoped, he would reverse his direction of influence and assist those he loved who were left living on earth while getting to know his daughter here better.

"Thank you, baba and ma. I guess I am coming home."

And Anoop felt like he already had. Paradise was a home of love and light with no drought of any kind in sight.

Chapter 21 – Oregon 2020

Conifer

"The best thing about rain forests is they never suffer from drought."- Dan Quayle

Pumpkins grown in Conifer's garden now adorned the Ridgeway's front porch. The few remaining would be carved as Jack-o-lanterns or baked into a pie. Conifer was not sure why his mother chose the pumpkins above all of his other harvested vegetables to represent the fall season. At least his pumpkins found their multiple purposes. Conifer enjoyed the cooler afternoon temperatures and the leaves changing colors, but he would miss the time spent growing things as he waited until next spring when he could begin planting again. The world was in the dying part of its cycle. During his garden's downtime, Conifer would take an agricultural break and focus his productive energies on the science project Neem felt was important for Conifer's future.

Neem suggested that they attempt to solve the problem droughts caused in the growing cycle. Irrigation used an original source of water to redirect where it was needed, which required a reliable constant source in fairly near proximity. Rainfall seemed the better option if it could be manipulated. It would be unreasonable to build huge structures to carry water long distances all over the world, Conifer pictured massive tubes crisscrossing the land like a huge waterslide park or a game of Mouse Trap. The Palestinians had done it anciently in the Middle East by building aquafers to carry water into their cities. The conquering Romans were advanced enough they must have figured out water relocation too, but those methods were still limiting.

He and Neem had discussed seeding clouds, but the dilemma continued on how to create clouds in the first place to direct the rainwater to whatever area of the globe needed it most. They must somehow perfect a process on how to create artificial clouds. Neem had joked that they would be creating the illusion of heaven on earth since a blanket of clouds was the traditional way heaven was often imagined or portrayed. This heavenly layer of clouds would also bless earthlings by weeping moisture onto the parched ground. Conifer hoped constructing clouds would also someday help create ever-ready rain forests to save the trees he loved. Their slogan could be "Have Clouds Will Rain."

Conifer practiced with simple experiments using alchemy, chemicals, and condensation. Today he had made a cloud in a jar. He read that clouds are formed when water vapor condenses into water droplets that attach to particles of dust, pollen, smoke, etcetera in the air. When billions of these water droplets join together, they form a cloud. Conifer poured warm water into a jar and swirled it around to warm the inside of the whole jar. Then he turned the lid upside down leaving it still on top of its container and placed several ice cubes into it. He quickly removed the ice carrying lid for a moment and sprayed some of his mom's aerosol hairspray into the jar. Thereby, introducing the contaminant particles needed to build a framework upon which the cloud could form. Wallah...he had a cloud. Conifer observed the embryo cloud for several minutes before opening the lid and watching it float away.

Conifer could hear Neem clapping, what must be his hands, followed by the words, "Looks like you have already started without me. Now you just need to repeat your efforts on a grander, but still controllable scale." When Conifer did not reply with even a thought, Neem continued, "I have been studying too. There are a few things necessary for clouds in the atmosphere to form. First moisture since there must be sufficient water vapor in the air. Then it needs cooling air where the air temperature must decrease enough for the water vapor to condense."

Conifer knew all of this but enjoyed collaborating with his friend so let Neem go on. "I watched young people do an experiment using shaving cream to create a small cloud on the top of the water, then they dropped food coloring onto it. As the shaving-cream-cloud filled up with the food coloring in it fell down into the water creating a rain-like effect. Your simulation is much more realistic and effective Conifer."

Finally, ready to communicate Conifer admitted, "I am not sure how we can get them high enough to work. Clouds are supposed to be at the upper reaches of the troposphere, which, depending on geographic location, occurs roughly between ten thousand and sixty thousand feet. Below that there are a few mid-level clouds, how high do you think ours need to be to work?"

"I wish I knew. I don't think the elevation matters really as long as we can deliver the rainwater where it needs to go. Man-made nature does not have to be an exact replica, but we can piggyback off of already existing principles. We do need to make sure to create the right kind of clouds. Whenever there is precipitation the clouds involved seem to be of the nimbus variety." Neem had done his homework too. "I also found that since 2010, a Dutch artist called Berndnaut Smilde has been skillfully creating clouds indoors. As strange as it might sound, Smilde has mastered the art of controlling the weather conditions of a room and can make clouds appear inside the oddest of spaces. I don't believe he seeds them for rain, but we might check out his work."

Puzzles requiring solutions intrigued Conifer and allowed him to feel what he imagined was close to joy. Then on top of that, he was able to work on this strategy, which might eventually be extremely useful, with Neem who understood him perfectly. The whole experience was unbelievably fulfilling. "Thank you for encouraging me towards this project Neem. Hopefully, between the two of us, we have the mental and physical resources needed to counteract lack of water around the world. Do you think we can accomplish it?"

"I have come to know that the best ideas are not necessarily from most intelligent minds, but from those who are the most in tune. You, my friend, are one who tunes in on a higher frequency," was Neem's cryptic response.

For over an hour Conifer and Neem brainstormed and applied various preliminary plans to accomplish their desired outcome. Their minds and spirits were in sync. Long before

Conifer was ready to end their time together, he heard his mother calling him to go with her to another *Matilda* practice. Conifer had no desire to go to the practice, he would much rather continue what he was working on with Neem. They were in a groove, but he felt Neem's presence withdraw with his mother's request. Conifer had yet to find a way to make his mother realize that Neem was a real person, until he did, she would never understand his desire to stay home and collaborate. He also sensed that for some unknown reason it meant very much to his mother that he be a part of her performance.

Brooke had initially tried to get him to play the part of Bruce Bogtrotter, a boy who ate a whole chocolate cake. Just the thought of being Bruce made Conifer shudder, there was no way that was happening. Then she offered to let him choose between the roles of Nigel, Tommy or Eric in the ensemble cast, but even their minor parts were beyond what Conifer felt comfortable with. He would prefer to watch the show from the audience, but his mom finally settled on letting him work behind the scenes helping Stetson with the sets and filling in with other backstage needs like lights, sound, and set changes. Both realized the mechanical side of the production was a better fit for him. Conifer was still supporting his mother's musical and that is what mattered.

"It's just you and me right now buddy, Juniper is still at the dog rescue and Stetson will bring her by after their shift is over," his mom answered without him even having to ask the question as they climbed into the car.

Conifer studied the clouds from the car window on their drive to the school. He found some cirrus and cumulus ones, but no nimbus floating by today. Hopefully, he would soon be able to unlock the secrets that were wrapped underneath their fluffy exteriors.

Several unfamiliar teens were milling around practice when they arrived. "I should have thought to request closed rehearsals," Brooke mumbled aloud. "Dang, I hope my actors don't shut down with an audience this soon. I guess we will see."

It was the Columbus Day holiday, so school was not in session, and Conifer surmised these students were not from his high school. An anxious feeling began to well up in his chest, Conifer attempted to push it down by digging into his assigned projects, but a weird tension in his head continued to increase. He gathered props and set up the stage for the opening scene. They were far enough into rehearsals that the actors who had lines were being microphoned so someone else was working on the sound system. His backstage jobs done, his director-mom asked him to sit out front where the audience would be on opening night and take notes on the lighting. She explicitly instructed him to watch for any faces that were in the dark or shadowed or anything else that needed to be enhanced and write down what needed to be changed. Conifer was not sure he would know what needed to be changed but he would do his best.

He noticed the extra students had migrated to the audience seats. Conifer carefully avoided their area of chairs as he sat down. The not-from-this-school students watched him as he concentrated on the lighting for each scene. A need to get up and pace poked at him but he had committed to checking the lights for his mother, so instead he rocked back and forth a little and repeated the words to the refrain of Taylor Swift's song *You Need to Calm Down* under his breath.

A few jeering comments pelted Conifer from the uninvited crowd.

"Hey, looks like that guy wishes he was on stage but didn't get a part," to a few guffaws.

"At least he has the rocking dance move down." Harsh laughter erupted all around.

The combination of the lights, music, movements on stage and taunts from the other teens all collapsed on Conifer. His brain was imploding or melting down and would soon cease to exist. A volcano fizzy drink was building up in his body. There was no ground, no air, no sky, just himself and fear, and desperation. His bones vibrated and splintered. His chest felt like it had been hooked up to a vacuum. He would wake with bruises and scrapes from grabbing onto anything, everything that might pull him back to earth. He was too big for his body, too big for this planet. Pain, like razor blades, scraped not over his skin, but over his soul.

Conifer sensed Juniper in his periphery. She was the normal twin, his better half. They were almost like Jekyll and Hyde. No, both Jekyll and Hyde were within him. It was like a switch flipped in his brain taking over his body, abolishing any rational thoughts, reactions, and communication. The blood in his head was pounding, and everything in it magnified more than his brain could hold or handle. There was a small section in the back of his brain that recognized what was going on and wanted to stop, but it couldn't override the system. Primal fight-or-flight was in high gear, instinctively he needed to isolate himself, to get anyway from other living forms of energy, but he could not speak or move. Where was Neem?

A crowd began to gather around the thrashing boy. Someone asked if he was having a seizure. Another unidentified voice which did not seem to be attached to anybody suggested that maybe they should call 911. With every ounce of control over his body that Conifer could muster he shook his head to signal "no". His mother was near him now, not physically containing him but verbally consoling. Then to the crowd, "he will be okay; I just need to get him home."

Yes, yes, his mother knew what was best for him. Lyrics from a Les Mis song filled his exploding brain but were frozen on this tongue, "*He's afraid, let him rest…bring him home, bring him home. Bring him peace, bring him joy, he is young, he is only a boy…Bring him home…*"

Stetson's calm voice of reason interjected, "Mrs. Ridgeway, I doubt you can leave all the students here without adult supervision. Juniper and I would be happy to bring him home."

Brooke appeared torn but accepted the offer, "Thank you Stetson. I will have the phone-tree start calling all the parents to let them know practice is over immediately and I will be home as soon as I can."

Memories of the ride home were a blur and would be erased by morning leaving only vague feelings in their place. Conifer was utterly exhausted as his sister helped him into their house. He just needed sleep. A warm furry body curled up beside him on his bed. Dr. Strange was the only physician whose physical contact or treatment Conifer welcomed right now.

Chapter 21 notes: Meltdowns are real for the ASD (Autism Spectrum Disorder) community due to sensory overload when too much sensory stimulus is occurring at once. It can be triggered by a crowded room, a TV turned up too loud, strong aromas, fluorescent lighting- or a hundred other things. Often, a meltdown is the only way to relieve the building tension of sensory overload. The outsider may perceive this as throwing a tantrum. After studying meltdown experiences of over twenty people with autism who were able to share verbal responses expressing what they were experiencing, I was able to piece together what might be going on in Conifer's head.

The cloud in a jar is a real experiment (as in the one with shaving cream) and the science behind cloud building is based on facts, but definitely mixed with fiction in my story. I am not a scientist so my reasoning may be flawed. Berndnaut Smilde has done some work on creating clouds indoors, but merely for artistic purposes. Real clouds form when warm air rises in the atmosphere and cools down. Cloud condensation nuclei, such as small particles of dust and pollution, enable water molecules to stick together and stop bouncing around. The water molecules condense around the nuclei to form clouds.

The four core types of clouds according to *Essay of the Modifications of Clouds* (1803) by Luke Howard divided clouds into three categories; cirrus (meaning curly or fibrous), cumulus (indicating heaped or piled) and stratus (suggesting sheets or layers). Then there are nimbus clouds which comes from the Latin word for rain.

Clouds are white because light from the sun is white. As light passes through a cloud, it interacts with the water droplets, which are much bigger than the atmospheric particles that exist in the sky. However, rain clouds are gray instead of white because of their thickness, or height. A cloud gets thicker and denser as it gathers more water droplets and ice crystals. The thicker it gets, the more light it scatters, resulting in less light penetrating all the way through it.

Conifer's song lyric from *Bring Him Home* by Colm Wilkinson

Chapter 22- NYC 2020

Blaze

*"It took a long time to get in a drought
and it won't take one overnight event to get us out."*
- Steve Bays

Now appeared to be the opportune time to tell Brooke about the assisted living plan for Conifer. Blaze had just listened over the phone to Brooke emotionally share what had happened during Conifer's recent meltdown and right in front of him on his desk lay the list Kylie had compiled of acceptable long-term living establishments for young adults with special needs. His nurturing wife should surely see the wisdom in his kind-hearted and concerned gesture at this juncture. Conifer was becoming too much for her to handle.

"Brooke, darling, I am so sorry that I am not nearer to be of more support at times like these," Blaze did not want to go in with guns *blazing*, a perfect pun if he did say so himself, "but I have been working on something that I believe will be the best solution for Conifer and for all of us."

"What are you talking about Blaze?" Brooke's voice sobered up immediately and took on an edge.

"Darling, Conifer is not going to get easier for you to handle as he becomes an adult man and we know how you feel about bringing him back to New York, so I have done some research," well Kylie had, but that was merely semantics. "There are several outstanding institutions around the country that offer living situations for people like our son. Even smaller adult group homes if you feel better about a more intimate environment for him. I know they are expensive, but we have the finances to keep him quite comfortable."

There was a long pause on the other end of the line before Brooke replied. "Why didn't I put this past you. Blaze you have never wanted an imperfect son around, but Conifer will be able to be independent one day, and if not, I refuse to have him institutionalized." The anger in Brooke's voice erupted through Blaze's end of their phone conversation. "Conifer just got overwhelmed at play practice. I should never have shared what happened with you and expected understanding."

Blaze's defensiveness caused him to let down his guard, "What kind of future can Conifer have, be realistic

Brooke. Do you plan to lead him around on a harness as a circus performer or maybe put him on some reality TV competition circuit? I heard an autistic blind boy won America's Got Talent by singing and playing the piano. I guess Conifer could be the rapping autistic boy." Blaze became a little too aggressive on the attack, which never went over well with Brooke.

"You're a piece of work Blaze Ridgeway. Why do I ever expect anything compassionate or at least human from you? Maybe because you are the boy's father..." Following those words, the call dropped.

Why were women always so irrational and emotionally based? Brooke would eventually think the situation through and realize he was right. Maybe this volunteer musical show that she was putting together was not such a good thing, it seemed to be making her more independent and withdrawn from him. He had married a passionate woman, perhaps all artists were. Blaze was still mulling over the Conifer issue when the other intense woman in his circle of influence entered his office with her business face on.

"Mr. Ridgeway, Blaze, I really need to discuss these numbers in your client portfolios. They do not seem to add up no matter how many different angles I go over them. It appears you are paying your long-term investors with the money from new investors and not from the investments themselves."

"Why, you're quite a little math whiz aren't you." The smile that formed on Blaze's thin lips did not extend to his eyes. "It would behoove you to remember that the big bucks I pay you are to keep the clients happy and paid, not to question where the investors' money comes from or goes to. At times I may do a little creative financing or shuffling of funds, but it all works out in the end. You don't need to worry your pretty little head about it." Blaze hoped the last comment did not come across condescending. He didn't need any workplace harassment issues, he had enough to deal with at the moment.

"I know what you pay my 'pretty little head' to do, but I also recognize a Ponzi scheme when I see one. Ponzi schemes happen to be illegal and I am not going down with you no matter how much you pay me."

The girl was even more attractive when she was all fired up. Too bad she was too smart for her own good. "I think there has been a misunderstanding Miss Taylor there is no investment fraud going on, I promise my clients high returns with little or no risk and that is what they are getting."

"So, you are telling me that you are actually investing their money in high yield adventures and not using it for other things?" Kylie pressed.

"For the most part. I have a reputation to maintain and client expectations to keep up. It is more complicated than I can currently explain, but there is no need for your concern, things will work out for the benefit of all, eventually." Blaze painted a positive face on the darker matter. Hopefully, it would all work out, at this point he was not completely sure.

Kylie did not look convinced. "I hope you are being straight with me. I deserve at least that much. If I find out differently, I will be giving my two-weeks' notice at the end of that very day."

Blaze was not sure if he had adequately redirected Kylie's concerns. The women in his life were being extremely difficult and unreasonable today. The worst part was, he was not sure that he could totally trust Kylie not to turn him in. She was such an ethical woman it would definitely be a conflict for her. He was only dabbling temporarily in the gray area of white-collar crime; he was not a fraudster. The financial downturn would rectify itself soon and he could return all his affairs to more legal order. But what was he to do in the meantime?

If he fired his assistant, she would be even more suspicious and have no reason not to turn him in for his minuscule misdeeds. He was not the kind of man who would entertain the idea of an untimely accident befalling his lovely co-worker or consider an assassin for hire, but the thought was slightly tempting. His life had become too messy and needed to be tidied up somehow. Maybe he could send Kylie on a paid vacation that would give him time to scrub his books better, but it was probably too late for that. And he currently didn't have the capital to make all of his client accounts balance legally as they should. It was like playing a game of Russian roulette wondering each day if the girl was going to turn him in or not. The rush could get his adrenaline flowing, but also be devastating if things turned south and she pulled the trigger.

Blaze needed to escape the confines of his office for a few minutes to clear his head. Leaving without a direction, purpose or a word to Kylie, he wandered Manhattan's streets blending in with the masses of humanity at home in his anonymity. Trinity Church where he had been married loomed ahead of him. General George Washington had gone there when elected president of this fledgling new nation seeking inspiration, perhaps Blaze could also seek sanctuary within its premises. After the 9-11 bombings, the small stone chapel had remained standing when more substantial structures around it had fallen. The building itself was a metaphor of hope.

Blaze entered through the fence's gates and roamed the cemetery surrounding Trinity Church. Famous names graced the headstones of several plots. Beneath his feet lay Alexander Hamilton buried beside his sister-in-law Angelica and not his wife Eliza, how strange. Hamilton was also a misunderstood American financial genius who was born into less than desirable lower-class family circumstances. Blaze could relate to the man. His tired legs gave out and he crumbled next to the ancient gravesite. It would be far more glamorous and icon worthy to go out of this world in a duel like Hamilton had rather than to be taken down by investor fraud. Unfortunately, he had no one specific in mind to challenge and the battle was within himself. Not to mention the fact that duels were also illegal, even in New Jersey. Blaze just sat there in the cemetery with a vacant mind for several minutes. Nothing came to him.

Finally, Blaze Ridgeway, not a man to be waylaid by his current setback, gathered strength from the revolutionary heroes surrounding him who had also faced insurmountable odds. He pulled himself back onto his own two feet and strode with his back straight and head held high out of the cemetery a renewed man. Blaze had not even entered the chapel but had received what he hadn't even realized he had come for - the strength to conquer whatever lay ahead.

Chapter 22 notes: The America's Got Talent winner in 2019 was Kodi Lee, a twenty-two-year-old, blind and autistic young man who was an extremely gifted musical savant. He received one million dollars by winning the hearts of America singing and playing the piano for millions.

Both pyramid and Ponzi schemes are illegal because they inevitably must fall apart. No program can recruit new members forever. Bernie Madoff operated the longest-running Ponzi scheme. For 20 years, investors poured $17.5 billion into his "investment firm" and with a net worth of only $300 million, Madoff was unable to reimburse them.

At Trinity Church, the graves and historical relevance surrounding the structure are all factual.

Chapter 23 – Oregon 2020

Juniper

"Like the modified monsoon. You flood my routine with so much love. Then leave me for so long that I wither in long emotional drought."- Harani B.

Celebration was in order. Juniper had passed her driving test this afternoon and tonight was going to the homecoming dance with the guy instrumental in making it happen. She held in her hand an official Oregon driver's license and the photo wasn't even half bad. Stetson should be proud of his star pupil. She got docked a few points on her less-than-perfect parallel parking and for going slightly into the other lane while avoiding a dog that looked like he was going to run in front of the car. Luckily, she still accumulated well above the amount needed to pass. Passing was a relief, but Juniper had to admit she would miss their practice sessions.

Tonight, would be Juniper's first-ever school dance and she was a little nervous. Brooke had taken Juniper to find an appropriate dress for the soiree. Juniper could not see herself in a long formal gown, so had selected instead, an above-the-knee, just below mid-thigh length, coral dress with lace overlay. The front was not low enough to show cleavage even if she had had any, but the back was scooped out below her shoulder blades with capped sleeves. The coral color was highlighted by her dark hair and it felt like the perfect orangish hue for a fall event. The dress was flattering on her figure but not too sexy. Hopefully, Stetson would approve.

As Juniper answered the door to his knock, she could see definite approval in Stetson's eyes. Her mother had offered to answer the door so Juniper could make a grand entrance but that was not her style.

"Wow, you look wonderful." Stetson gushed.

"You clean up pretty good yourself." Juniper smiled. Stetson did look sharp in his black slim-fit slacks with black, long-sleeved, button-up shirt and a skinny coral tie. He had asked what color she was wearing and had made an extra effort to match her. "I have good news for you too. I passed my driving test today."

With unbridled enthusiasm Stetson impetuously grabbed Juniper around the waste, swept her off her feet and swung her around, then quickly set her back down making sure he had not crushed the flowers he brought with him.

"Already warming up for the dance I see," Brooke teased as she walked into the room.

"Sorry, just happy Juniper passed her driving test," Stetson stammered uncharacteristically as he handed Brooke a small bouquet of mixed flowers. "These are for you, Mrs. Ridgeway… and this is for you Juniper," as he slid a semi-smooshed corsage of small coral rosebuds around Juniper's slender wrist. "I hope you both like them."

Both women simultaneously said, "thank you." Then Brooke added, "you are quite the gentleman tonight Mr. Buttars. I greatly appreciate being remembered with flowers too."

Juniper was impressed that Stetson thought to include her mother, her date was both thoughtful and smooth.

"Well, we better be off. I made reservations at the Pine Tavern to go to dinner before the dance with a few other couples. Conifer are you sure you don't want to join us?" Stetson called to Juniper's brother across the room.

Conifer who still had not totally recovered from the previous incident with the kids presumed to be from Stetson's school shook his head a convincing "no".

"Conifer and I have our own date night planned. Dinner from his favorite burger joint, then a movie and popcorn here at home," Brooke shared. "Thanks again for the flowers."

Juniper felt like she was in a fairytale on the arm of a handsome prince as they entered the restaurant. A tall pine tree grew up through a hole in the floor and out of the roof in the middle of the dining area. Large glass windows overlooked a smooth, tree-encompassed body of water. Conifer would love this place; she and her mother would have to bring him back here for a special occasion another time. The food was fancy and delicious. Stetson even ordered a mud pie for them to split for dessert without even knowing it was one of her favorites. The other couples were inclusive enough. Juniper did not really know any of them well; the guys were buddies of Stetson and everyone in the group were in grades ahead of her at Bend High. She had seen most of them at school, and they didn't make her feel awkward for being the youngest in the party.

At the dance, the fairytale continued even without a godmother. The twinkle lights strung across the ceiling above the forest-themed décor was enhanced by music with rhythmical beats. The entwined effect was magical. She and Stetson were both decent dancers and had fun during the night mimicking many of the classic old dance steps from the Sprinkler and Funky Chicken to the Macarena, ending up with the more recent Floss dance move. They even convinced the DJ to play a shortened version of Michael Jackson's song *Thriller* so they could encourage the wallflower students sitting on the sidelines to get up and moving in the ghoulish group dance.

During the very few slow dance songs that the DJ played; Juniper's heart was beating so loudly in her chest she was pretty sure Stetson must be able to hear it. She thought she could feel his beating rapidly as well as he put one arm around her waist and pulled her in close. Juniper lay her head against his thumping chest and felt like she never wanted the night to end. Were they becoming a couple? If so, she would make sure there was more talking than kissing when they were together. Juniper intended for Stetson to like her for her brain more than her body, though she knew neither were anything to brag about. How did a person know when they were in love with someone? She didn't think they were close to that yet, but there may be potential. Stetson was the kind of guy she would want to end up with one day in the distant future. He was nothing like her father.

The only blight of the night was when Stetson drug Juniper off the dance floor to get some punch before they both became dehydrated. An old girlfriend sauntered by and asked Stetson for a dance. He was too nice to blatantly refuse, so asked Juniper if it was okay with her. What was Juniper to say? With either answer, she would lose something - either a dance with her date or her dignity as she came across as the jealous girlfriend. So, she watched her prince dance away with his past love wanting to pull out every hair of the girl's coiffed blonde bun and wishing she had had the courage to just say no. Stetson was hers for the night.

It was all over before it had barely begun, and they were standing on her front porch for the traditional goodnight kiss. Juniper had gained a few skills in that area during the past few months. Their lips hungrily found each other and worked in sync to heighten their emotions and put an exclamation mark on the end of the memorable night. She pulled away before either of them was ready but before it became too late for either to stop.

"I had the best time tonight Stetson, thank you for everything. Really." It hardly seemed enough to say with all she was feeling inside.

Stetson gazed into her eyes awkwardly long. "You really are something, Juniper Ridgeway. I'm glad you don't know how great you are, or I would never have a chance." Then with another quick peck, her prince (who had not been changed from a frog by her kiss) hopped off the steps in one big jump and headed to his car without her glass slipper.

Juniper floated through the front door towards her bedroom. The lights were off, but her mother called from another bedroom to inquire how the night had gone. Juniper attempted to paint the picture of her perfect night; however, mere words could not do it justice. Dr. Strange wandered out of Conifer's room to greet her on her way down the hall. So odd that her dog seemed to prefer her brother who did not even really like animals. She had definitely named the pup accurately…the dog was a strange one, he preferred the unusual over the more mundane. Perhaps he had a sixth sense that let him know where he was needed. Or maybe he was actually a psychiatric doctor and not a medical one at all – ha-ha. Of course, with his superpowers, he could be both.

She was in such a delightful mood Juniper didn't want to end the night just yet. She doubted she could sleep even if she tried and reliving the real thing was better than any dream her unconscious mind may come up with. The rest of her living family may have gone to bed, but she could hang out with her dead ones on Ancestry for a while until she felt drowsy. Juniper was getting pretty proficient at searching records on the website.

She fired up the laptop and returned to her most recent search efforts. Juniper had figured out on her last trip into the past researching names that John Fountain was not an uncle after all, but her sixth great grandfather. She had been confused and missed the direct connection because her mom's ancestor line remained rooted in Great Britain and she had known that John departed for India on a mission. What she had consequently uncovered was that after living in India, for who knew how long, John's wife Hannah must not have been able to hack it, or for some other unknown reason, she had taken all of their children back to Great Britain to be raised there. Including her son Matthew who became another of Juniper's eventual great grandpas. His father John stayed in India to serve his mission until he died years later.

Tonight, she was randomly scanning through whatever information she could find on the Fountain family tree during that approximate time period. It was not a precise science, but Juniper found it an enjoyable pastime. She liked knowing about the people whose genetics made her who she was. Finally, she found a nugget of information that was a priceless gem in her hunt. It appeared that a brother of grandpa Matthew remained in India with his father John and did not return to England when the rest of his family did. Juniper wondered who this boy was and what became of him. Finding census lists or marriage, birth and death records from India was much more difficult than recovering them from English archives.

More fascinated by possible Indian cousins than her direct line of European ancestors, Juniper kept digging. Bingo. There he was in black and white on her screen. Tristan Fountain, son of John Fountain was employed by the British East India Trading Company from the mid to late 1800s. Why hadn't he gone back to England with his mother? Had Uncle Tristan ever married or produced children? Were there descendants of brave Uncle Tristan still living in India? If so, who were they and where were they? Her late-night internet browsing had done exactly the opposite of what she had intended it to. Now Juniper would have even more trouble shutting down her hyped-up brain, let alone her laptop. Both new boyfriend Stetson and long-lost cousin Tristan would be occupying major space in her cluttered mind, dancing their way through her sleepless thoughts and with any luck eventually waltzing her into incredible dreams.

Chapter 23 notes: There is a Pine Tavern in Bend, Oregon with a pine tree that grows up through the middle of the restaurant and goes out through the roof. It overlooks Mirror Pond on the Deschutes River.

Chapter 24 – Paradise/Oregon 2020

Anoop/Neem

"Droughts and difficulties are reality for all of us.
When the dry of your drought is fierce,
God is inviting you to serve and trust Him
in the arid, arduous trenches of it.
You are not alone."- Gwen Smith

Anoop settled into Paradise over several decades of earth time reckoning. His perspective from this vantage point was much clearer. Many things he had thought were tragedies in his days on earth, he could see had been blessings in disguise. Yes, at times, he did witness great wickedness that must bring even the Supreme Being to tears, yet he saw acts of great love every day as well. Just yesterday he watched a young expectant mother refuse treatment that would save her life to allow time for the child within her to grow and live a life of its own. That kind of ultimate sacrifice made Anoop weep.

He reflected on several assignments where he had spent time during this century and hoped he had made a difference in some mortal lives. During the 1950s on earth, most of his focus had been directed towards the family he left behind on the farm, inspiring them on how to survive day by day. When the '60s hit Anoop began to branch out over the world letting his heart be his guide as to where best to invest his celestial energies.

The Vietnam War was a nasty affair and Anoop hoovered over that country lending solace to soldiers and civilians alike as he could. The United States of America was full of unrest with civil rights protests, and the assassinations of both President John F. Kennedy and Martin Luther King. Others spent time inspiring Americans through their trials, but the most exciting assignment passed out was probably given to those who helped the first man land on the moon. Mortals were always trying to get a little closer to heaven in whatever way they could.

During the following decade, the U.S. signed a peace pact and their troops pulled out of Vietnam, but a war between his own home country and Pakistan began. A huge gulf remained between their two countries stemming from their religious differences and the division created when Great Britain withdrew. Remnants of that conflict were still going on today. One of his grandsons fought in their country's battle and Anoop stayed near this boy's side nearly the whole time he was involved. War was a constant somewhere on the earth. Israel and the Arab states were always in conflict.

Anoop saw great highs and lows being played out before him. Horrendously, a cult leader in Jonestown, Guyana convinced his followers to commit mass suicide and abortions of unborn babies became legal. Great advances in technology were taking place at the same time too. Genetically engineered insulin became available to those suffering from diabetes and the mobile phone was invented. Anoop had yet to determine if the cell phone was a blessing or a curse.

In the 1980s India's Prime Minister Indira Gandhi was assassinated by two Sikh bodyguards and a thousand Sikhs were killed in riots. Indira's son Rajiv Gandhi succeeded his mother. As a Sikh, he knew they were considered warriors, but warriors to protect their people against enemies from the outside and not attack within. Anoop chose to stay close to his homeland during this decade trying to the heal hearts of his countrymen. More tragedy struck his earthly home ground when a toxic gas leak from a chemical plant in Bhopal, India killed two thousand and injured one hundred and fifty thousand. Then an explosion in the Chernobyl nuclear power plant in the former USSR was even worse and spread radiation over much of Russia and Europe. The most hopeful thing to happen in the 80s was when the Berlin wall separating communism from the western world was torn down.

Anoop knew that time was inconsequential, but it helped him organize in his mind the events of the world by using their method of marking it pass. The saddest and most devastating place he served in the 1990s was in Africa during the Rwandan genocide. Man's inhumanity to man almost extinguished his hope there. Then at a high school in the USA called Columbine, two teenagers shot and killed fifteen students including themselves; that country had been plagued with school shootings ever since. People attempted to seek notoriety for both good and bad deeds. With the world population reaching six billion by the end of the decade, Anoop began focusing on helping more people choose good deeds.

The dawn of a new century brought more of the same... wars, contention, shootings, but social media also arrived on the scene with a networking website called Facebook. Instead of making the people of the world more social it seemed to have the opposite effect. Many humans no longer took the time to reach out personally and contact one another. They posted staged pictures portraying perfect lives and shared their political leanings. Contentions and depressions increased.

Anoop had recently been drawn to assist a distant relative, one who needed him more than any other at this moment in the history of the world. The young man was trapped inside himself and had difficulty communicating with others but for some reason, he effortlessly heard Anoop. Their across-dimension connection was easier than it had ever been with anyone before. The boy was very bright, he just needed a boost of confidence with his self-esteem. Anoop offered the young man his metaphorical hand, through impressions from his mind, to hold onto as the teen figured out his lack of limitations.

The two had been working on a project together, one that would not only help the youth get into college but also be a blessing for the world. The boy had never asked Anoop who he was or where he came from. He had accepted Anoop's presence as a normal manifestation and not questioned his intentions. Anoop was getting a strong impression that part of his mission included letting the teen know of their distant family relationship. Today was his unveiling.

When Anoop arrived, the young man was sitting on his sofa with headphones covering his ears absorbing some sort of textbook with his eyes. His thirst for knowledge was insatiable.

"Good morning Conifer, are you ready to go to work?" The boy sensed Anoop's presence immediately and a smile spread across his usually serious face. "Before we get going on the science fair project, I wanted to have a more personal discussion with you. Have you ever wondered who I was? You've never asked my name?"

"I thought you would tell me if you wanted me to know. I call you Neem after a tree that is helpful to mankind - like you are to me. My name is a tree too." Conifer admitted.

"That is a nice name, but my real name is Anoop. I am one of your ancestors who lived on the earth a hundred years ago. Some of our family lost their lives during that time due to drought, but I lived a long life despite the difficult conditions."

"Is that why you want to fix it, fix the lack of rain?" Conifer did not seem shocked by the revelation.

"Partly and also because I feel a connection to you, Conifer."

"Are you an angel?

"Some people call us by that name. I have already lived my life on this earth. But since you have a scientific mind, you understand that matter does not die. Matter cannot

221

be created or destroyed just rearranged into different shapes and consistencies to fulfill different purposes, like with the breakdown of elements in the soil. I was once a man like you are now, but my matter has been transformed and I am fulfilling another purpose. My current purpose is to help you…my many times' great-nephew or perhaps cousin. I'm afraid your sister is better at genealogy than I am, we share a grandfather named John Fountain. I want to help you let others understand how much you have hidden inside that head of yours. Together we can put your brainpower to work. You can make a difference in the world, one that I wasn't able to when I was here." Anoop explained.

"Will I be like you one day?" Conifer questioned.

"I believe so."

"Why am I this way now?"

"What do you mean?"

"Why does my brain get so cluttered sometimes I cannot bear it and it feels like it is going to explode? And why are my words all stuck in my head so I can only express myself with words from songs?" Conifer pleaded to know.

"I do not have the wisdom to understand everything, but I have learned that everyone on earth is given challenges to overcome. Some are easier to see than others. All of my sisters and my brother died from a disease we did not even have a name for. And my mother passed away from starvation due to lack of enough rainfall for our crop to grow. Today, you can turn on a faucet and have water whenever you desire it and you have access to excess food that is lined up on shelves at your markets. Few go hungry. Things are more equal than they appear."

"Will I still be like this when I am where you are? Conifer asked Anoop.

"You will still be you, but a perfect version of you. All of the things that you struggle with now will be erased. I believe your speaking situation will continue to improve while you are here on earth, but communication in paradise is very similar to how we are talking together right now, so either way, you will not have a problem." Anoop was not sure how much to share of the world beyond the one Conifer knew.

"Thank you for being my friend." Conifer's sincerity melted Anoop's heart, validating all of his efforts. "How can I let my mom know you are real?"

"Most people on earth cannot hear us as you can Conifer. They attribute our words in their minds as coming from their own thoughts. Your mother may never believe I am here. You are a special young man with higher gifts."

"You mean I have a superpower, like Dr. Strange" Conifer wondered.

"Yes, you definitely have a superpower Conifer." Dr. Strange had perked up his ears in response to the mental mention of his name. Perhaps the pup was endowed with gifts as well. Most animals seemed to be extra intuitive to beings from Anoop's dimension. Pride and the rules of reality did not get in their way.

"Can I see you, please? See what you look like?" Conifer unexpectedly inquired.

Anoop was caught off guard, no one he assisted had ever asked to see him. He knew of others in paradise who had appeared to people on earth for various reasons. "Some people are able to see us, and others cannot. I will do what I can to make it happen for you." Anoop switched his concentration from verbal communication to physical manifestation. He would not look the same as a physical human being, his form would appear more translucent, only visible to some human eyes. Anoop turned inward to become seen outward.

"I can see you. I can really see you! Thank you, Neem, I mean Anoop." Conifer marveled, his joy tangible. "Your skin is darker than mine but glows like there is light underneath it. Is everyone beautiful in your world?"

"I suppose so. We are beings of more light. Light makes things glorious."

Brooke Ridgeway entered the room as Anoop glowed visibly before Conifer, but the boy's mother was obviously unaware of Anoop's presence.

"Conifer is everything okay? You seem so happy," the woman did notice the difference in her son but had no idea the source of his joy.

"Help me let her see you," Conifer begged Anoop, but Conifer's valiant verbal attempt to call Anoop's presence to his mother came out, *"Snoop (Anoop) Dog... You're in the arms of the angel, may you find some comfort here."*

"Yes, you are my angel, cute boy, thank you for wanting to give me comfort. And the dog already has a name, however, Snoop Dog would be a clever one." Brooke had totally misinterpreted her son's message. Conifer's disappointment was tangible.

"Don't give up my boy, things will be okay," Anoop mentally soothed Conifer as his own physical presence dissolved before the boy's eyes. "We will keep working on your science fair project and your mother and others will at least see who you really are."

Chapter 24 notes: The world events that Anoop witnessed through the decades are all factual.

Conifer's song lyric is *Angel* by Sara McLachlan, also Snoop Dog is a modern-day rapper.

Chapter 25 – Oregon 2020

Brooke/Blaze

"The drought was the very worst when the flowers that we'd grown together died of thirst." -Taylor Swift

Snow fell on Bend, Oregon. The Cascade mountain range to the west was blanketed with the white fluff and Mount Bachelor was dotted with skiers. The Ridgeway's were not skiers, but Brooke had bundled up the family for a little sledding adventure. Blaze was home for the whole week, and she needed to get him out of the house. The man still found plenty to complain about out in the cold surrounded by all of winter's glory.

"If you are going to live next to these mountains why don't you have the kids skiing by now and not just slip-sliding down this kiddy hill. And where is the lodge to go get some hot cocoa or something a little stronger to warm us up?" Blaze scanned the area totally missing nature's frosted beauty in his midst.

"I brought a thermos, it's in the car," Brooke shared. "I'll go get it."

"I think we are all ready to go anyway," Blaze answered for everyone.

It wasn't worth arguing with him, so Brooke began gathering up the innertube and snow disk to pack away in the car. Blaze had come to Oregon to see *Matilda* and stay through Christmas. He rarely stayed this long. Brooke knew she should be pleased by his effort to support her but couldn't help wondering if he was here fulfilling his duty or avoiding something back in New York. Nothing in Bend seemed to please him. The musical was not an exception.

Last night before the show Mr. Martinelli had taken both of Brooke's hands in his as he sincerely thanked her for pulling off the miracle they were about to witness. Then parted the stage curtain and walking through to introduce the impending performance to the waiting audience. The man was a class act and his belief in Brooke had stilled her anxious nerves. She was glad he thanked her before the performance began, who knew how the actual show would go and she had been so excited about bringing *Matilda* to life on the stage she doubted she could have faced her benefactor afterward if the outcome had been a total disaster. Brooke knew the cast had obvious limits, but the student actors had been pretty amazing within their autistic range. Her hopes were high.

The house lights dimmed as Principal Martinelli exited the stage and the curtains opened onto the first scene. It may not have gone off without a hitch, but through Brooke's eyes, it was pretty magical. The girl who played Matilda captured her part nearly perfectly - quirky with a sensitive strength. Brooke could not have asked for anything more. And the boy who played Matilda's father Harry Wormwood was hysterical whether intended or not. Humor is not usually a strength on the spectrum.

There were a few mishaps but that was to be expected in an amateur performance. Brooke cast the largest boy who tried out in the role of Miss Trunchbull the huge, bullying principal which was often done to add to the illusion and the humor of the part. However, the young man kept forgetting he was supposed to be playing a woman, he kept missing his cues or changing his lines to make them relevant to his gender. The autistic world is extremely literal. It had been a mistake on Brooke's part to expect so much of the student. Then another boy playing Bruce Bogtrotter ate so much chocolate cake so quickly that he threw it all back up onto the stage. Brooke was fairly sure that his nerves also played a big part in the upheaval. Most of the audience wouldn't know that vomiting was not actually in the script, so they just went with it. More mess for the stage crew to clean up, but her team graciously pulled off the improv eruption.

Conifer did not miss a beat in his backstage scene setups. After his meltdown during rehearsal, while out front assessing the lighting, Brooke kept Conifer carefully hidden behind the scenes. Every prop was present, and every scene change performed swiftly with items correctly placed. Conifer was a Rockstar. Juniper was Brooke's right hand, making sure every cast member was in their place ready to go on stage when it was their time to perform and whispering their lines behind the curtain whenever anyone forgot. Juniper was subtle with her assistance making sure not to lessen the overall effect of the student's participation.

By the time Mr. Wormwood agreed to let Matilda live with Miss Honey and the whole cast began singing the reprise to *When I Grow Up*, Brooke could finally breathe. She realized what an overachieving accomplishment they had all pulled off and took her first full breath since the show began, maybe since the first practice started. It may not have been a flawless performance but even the little foibles added to the musical's charm. With the closing bows, the whole audience was on their feet clapping wildly. The Oak Leaf Academy theater department had a successful show under their belts.

The cast may not be ready for a U.S. tour, but perhaps they would hold an encore performance after the holidays.

Blaze had been somewhat supportive after the play as parents lined up to convey their surprise and appreciation in the quality of the performance. Her smiling husband kept his hand strategically placed on her shoulder but made snide comments into Brooke's ear to ensure she knew he thought she could do better, and that autistic theater was a bit beneath her. Brooke felt exactly the opposite. She had used her skills to create something she and others enjoyed while participating in something she loved and at the same time she had hopefully made a difference within the neglected community her son was a part of. Brooke felt it was one of the greatest accomplishments of her life and was already pondering appropriate musicals to attempt another show again next year with this troupe of actors, assuming Principal Martinelli asked her back. His added gratitude after the show's completion led her to believe that he was planning on continuing the theater program.

Winter break began the day following *Matilda*, so the musical performance was an early Christmas present from those involved given to their school and their parents. The gift may not be wrapped with a bow, but it was priceless. Tonight, was Christmas Eve as the Ridgeway's returned home from the sledding hill.

The family of four sat in front of the fire and started their annual rituals for the evening. First, they consumed a nice meal together, this year Brooke decided to forego all the cooking and ordered in Indian food. It was ethnically delicious and left few dishes to be washed. Afterward, they started the night off by playing at least one game as a family. This year Juniper suggested charades with all Christmas themed songs or movies to act out so Conifer could play more easily. Brooke drew *Rock Around the Christmas Tree* which ended up being easier to guess than she supposed it might be. Blaze appropriately drew *The Grinch who Stole Christmas* and barely had to act his out. Juniper used Dr. Strange, even though props were against the rules, to get them all to guess *Rudolf the Red-Nosed Reindeer.* Conifer went last but they guessed his the fastest. He placed his hand over his mouth and then both hands beside his head to make a pillow and his sister shouted out *Silent Night.* It must be a twin thing because Brooke would never have gotten it that quickly.

Next, they sang a few Christmas carols in awkward four-part harmony- soprano, alto, bass, and spoken-rap. The mood in the room was sweet as Brooke read from the book of Luke chapter two in the New Testament before they each got to open one present. Brooke had borrowed the tradition of opening one gift on Christmas Eve from her childhood home and her children looked forward to it every year.

Juniper picked first since she was the youngest by a few minutes. She chose to open her gift from Conifer and let out a little squeal when she found a dog-shaped keychain inside holding her own set of car keys. He was proud that his sister had gotten her driver's license and since she was not getting her own car from him or her parents anytime in the near future, this made her feel like an official driver carrying her own set of keys.

Conifer returned the act and selected the gift from Juniper to open. She had not been as creative as her brother. Inside lay a twenty-five-dollar gift card, the amount of their imposed gift limit, to iTunes for Conifer to download some of his favorite songs onto his phone. Conifer gave his sister another gift by giving her a hug for her efforts. Hugs were hard for him, so the sacrifice meant a lot.

Brooke went next and Blaze insisted she open the gift from him. For some reason getting gifts from Blaze always made her nervous. The small package was professionally wrapped, unlike the homespun jobs on the previous two packages. Brooke lifted off the lid of the smaller sized box, it looked a little too large to contain jewelry. Inside lay two airline tickets to Paris with a note explaining that they could be exchanged for two weeks' vacation to any location of her choosing in the next two months. Brooke was not sure how to respond. A vacation, of course, was wonderful, but there were only two tickets in the package, not four. What would she do with Conifer? He was really too old for a babysitter and too much responsibility for his sister.

Realizing she had not responded Brooke finally spoke, "This is a fun and generous gift Blaze, we can talk about it later. Thank you so much."

Her lack of instant enthusiasm and failure to squeal like Juniper had over the key chain gift obviously disappointed Blaze. "Why not now? Where would you like to go Brooke? We both deserve a vacation. It has been years and the kids are old enough to leave home alone."

If she shared her real feelings right now, the night would end in an argument. "You are right, but I am not sure it is really a good time."

"It is never a good time is it Brooke. You can never leave your precious son. Maybe I should give him my gift a few years early. Guess what Conifer boy, I have found a home for you when you graduate. Cannot live with mommy forever now can you."

"Stop it, Blaze. Not tonight." Brooke pleaded.

233

"Geez, dad, trying to act out your Grinch charade again?" Juniper quipped. "Come on Conifer, let's go in the other room and watch *Home Alone* and wish we were home alone while our loving parents figure their gift out. Merry Christmas to us."

Brooke did not want to have this conversation now. It was Christmas Eve. She knew she should want to go with her husband on a wonderful trip, but she was torn. "I'm sorry Blaze. Your gift is super sweet; can we just wait a little longer to go? And you know how I feel about your other idea. That will never happen."

"Longer like a few more weeks, or few more years, or few more decades? I'm getting tired of waiting for you Brooke. At some point, you are going to have to choose between the two men in your life."

"I do not plan to put Conifer in an institution even if he doesn't go to college, he is quite intelligent Blaze and he will be able to accomplish so much on his own. If you would ever give him a chance!"

"It appears you have already made your decision. I will see if I can get a flight out tonight or the first thing in the morning." Blaze spoke without emotion.

"But…it is Christmas, Blaze." Then Brooke bit her tongue. Their Christmas celebration may be better for everyone if he left.

"I guess this is another gift to you." Then pulled out his cell phone to call the airline.

Blaze was able to get a great price on the last-minute flight since it was leaving so early on Christmas morning. The kids had not even woken up to check their stockings when the uber picked him up to take him to the airport. His plane ticket present to Brooke had been a test. If Brooke was willing to go away with him for a few weeks he would plan their future lives going forward together. If she could not leave her twins for that brief stretch of time, it was doubtful that she would ever separate herself from them for him. He would have to plan for his future as a single man. He had changed his identity before. It was not that hard. It would have been nice to take his wife with him into a new life but starting over as a wealthy eligible bachelor had its advantages too. He just needed to decide who he would become next and what area of the world was calling him…Europe, South America or perhaps on an island somewhere in Indonesia. He did not plan to go to prison, even a white-collar one.

Blaze had socked away enough of a nest egg to live in style anywhere he landed, with enough money left over to leave a little for Brooke and the kiddos, so they would be financially okay too. She would not live a life of luxury, but that was not her style anyway. If he could somehow pull off an accident to make it look like he was dead, she could even get the dividend from his life insurance policy and be quite comfortable. There was a part of him that hated to start over all alone again. Blaze briefly wondered if Juniper would want to go with him instead. The girl seemed the most likely to up for an adventure out of all of the eligible candidates in his life, but the reality of staying incognito with a teenage sidekick shot down that tempting idea almost immediately.

Of course, he would not leave until he knew for sure the noose was closing around his neck, but he would be prepared for a quick exit at any moment. Wouldn't it be ironic if he got his foot caught in the door, before he could get away, and he ended up heading to the same prison his father was in? Bobby and Dickie could catch up on all the father/son moments they had missed out on through the years. In reality, Bobby Minor was probably paroled by now, if not dead. Blaze wondered if Brooke would visit him in the Upstate Correctional prison if the worst-case scenario befell him.

The pilot announced over the plane's intercom system to prepare for final landing. Then added, "And Merry Christmas to the passengers of United flight #1225 Portland to New York City. Thank you for flying with us on your holiday." It had been a long day, there were no direct flights out of the Redmond airport, so he endured a layover. Blaze felt like he was living the Christmas movie *Home Alone* that his kids were watching last night, but the second one- *Home Alone 2: Lost in New York*. Maybe he would book a room at the Plaza Hotel for the night like the Kevin kid did.

Chapter 25 notes: There is a Mount Bachelor ski resort in Bend, Oregon.

Chapter 26 - Oregon 2021

Conifer

"You see, I had been riding with the storm clouds, and had come to earth as rain, and it was drought that I had killed with the power that the Six Grandfathers gave me."
- Black Elk

Conifer rarely spoke lately, even in lyrics. His father's brutal announcement on Christmas Eve sharing Conifer's impending institutional placement had knocked out any ounce of confidence he may have had in verbal attempts. Anoop, formally known as Neem, still visited regularly to extend friendship and help Conifer with his science fair project. Sometimes Conifer wondered what the point was, but he didn't want to disappoint the one male figure in his life that did believe in him.

They had gone over all the facts repeatedly and practiced reading or pointing out all the main points on the posters Juniper had helped him make. Juniper was much more skilled at graphic arts than Conifer was and Anoop had issues holding a writing utensil in this dimension. There was probably a way Anoop could make it work, but Juniper was here and happy to help.

Today was the district science fair. Since there were only two Oak Leaf Academy students interested in participating, the district had allowed them to skip the first round at their own school and enter the competition on the district level. Those who placed in the top spots here would go on to the state science fair in Portland. Conifer had to miss school for the day to participate. Most students would think that was cool, but Conifer hated to miss a single day of school. He got behind in his studies and had makeup homework assignments to complete. Nevertheless, here he was at Bend High School.

The memories of the students from this school who had contributed to his meltdown made Conifer nervous, so his mom was there, sitting on a chair not in his booth area but close enough to be available in an instant should he need her. The gymnasium was closed off and monitored so people could not wander through unless they were supposed to be involved. This afternoon session was only for the judges and tonight the science fair would be open for public viewing. Somehow Juniper slipped past the safety net to swing by and say hello.

"Hey, my posters look sharp, don't they? How d'you like my school? Think you might want to transfer here and share some of your super-smarts with us average students next year?" Then picking up on Conifer's anxious vibes by his complete silence, Juniper added, "No worries big bro, you are going to slay it. Truly. Just breathe."

Conifer felt very prepared and confident with his scientific hypothesis and the data that he and Anoop had researched. The presentation side was another story. Anoop promised to be there for backup support and told Conifer that everything he needed to say for the presentation was on the poster boards, so he didn't need to fret. Fret must have been an olden time word. Conifer had to look it up.

He was using Berndnaut Smidle's method of creating a cloud in a room to impress and maybe even shock the judges. Then half of the wall behind him was dedicated to the known procedure of seeding clouds, the other half to his cloud formation formula. "Death to Drought" was the main title of his science fair presentation and was stretched across the top of the dividers in large black font. Hanging below on his posters was the slogan "make clouds - create rain".

Conifer was situated next to a project about electricity with a balloon and comb on the student's table to show how static electricity was created, then a second step had all sorts of objects to determine the best conductors of electricity. On the other side of him was a girl beneath a sign that read "Racing Bristlebots: on your mark, get set, GO!" She had built her very own robots from scratch using the head of a toothbrush, a battery, and a small motor. Once completed, they buzzed along the top of a table like bugs. Her project was impressive. Across from him was "A Battery that makes Cents". The student's poster said that batteries are expensive, but that you can make one of your own for exactly twenty-four cents. Using a voltaic pile, the boy had built a battery composed of pennies and nickels. Conifer hoped his project was interesting enough to compete.

The judges had begun making their rounds looking over all the projects and listening to the presentations. Where was Anoop? Conifer listened to the girl next to him explain bristlebot racing and started to feel the familiar buzz in his head. Please don't let him have a meltdown today. He did not see any of the students from the *Matilda* rehearsal, and all of the budding scientists around him seemed nice, but the pressure was beginning to build. Before Conifer was ready, two men and a woman sat down in front of his designated area, smiled at him, and asked him to share his research. They were ready.

Without speaking Conifer began to create the cloud he and Anoop had practiced. His silence allowed the judges to focus solely on the actual science that was taking place. Conifer heard a few "oohs" and "awes" as a cloud took shape and floated before them. It was pretty impressive if Conifer did say so, or at least think so, himself. During the next part of the presentation, Conifer followed his scripted posters as planned, reading aloud the words his sister had carefully written on them for him. He was almost home free when one of the judges asked Conifer a question.

"Do you believe your project could have global implications?"

Conifer pointed to the answer on the sign and read it off robotically. He must sound like one of the bristlebots would if they could talk.

Then the woman judge asked him another question that was not on the printed script. "Why did you select this project Conifer? Does it play any personal place in your life?"

This was not a part of the pre-written presentation. Conifer could feel the fog of panic begin to creep in. Where was Anoop?? He ran some songs lyric through his head... *"because I'm happy, clap along if you feel like a room without a roof."* His project did make him happy, but he had not chosen it because he was happy. No, this song would not quite work. How about *"Don't worry, be happy"*. Bob Marley's song was better, but still not quite right, choosing this subject had more to do with supporting his family members who had gone through drought and preventing it from ever happening again regardless of it making him happy personally.

What about *"we are family, I got all my sister(s) with me"*. Maybe the judges would think he was artistically expressing that the world was a family. Conifer was about ready to let these lyrics rap out of his mouth when he felt Anoop arrive, Anoop's calming presence flooded Conifer.

"I am sorry to be late my friend. You have been doing awesome on your own. Just relax and repeat the words I put into your thoughts." With Anoop's reassurance, the mist filling Conifer's mind started to clear and evaporate into the cloud floating above their heads.

"I love to plant and grow things, so originally considered a project growing trees." Conifer repeated Anoop's word aloud. The words were true, why hadn't he been able to come up with them. "Recently, I discovered some of my family members who lived in the previous century also liked to grow things," he paused to hear the rest of the sentence, "but they were plagued by long timespans with no rainfall that created drought in their area." This was also true and not so hard to share. "In fact, a few of those related to me even lost their lives because of famine caused by drought." Conifer could feel the emotion of the words he was saying as well as the sadness Anoop was feeling. Empathic tears formed in Conifer's eyes. That had never happened before. Conifer could perceive Anoop's pain in losing his mother due to the dry conditions.

At that moment all of Conifer's own limitations fled from his head, his concern and focus were on his new friend and the tragedies Anoop had experienced during his lifetime. Words began to form in Conifer's mind and haltingly spilled out of his mouth. "I care about a relative who has been assisting me with my work." Hopefully, the judges would not ask to see Anoop, his mother had not been able to. That would involve a different kind of experiment. "He lost his mother. I don't want anyone I love to ever have to feel that sad again." Conifer knew that he truly didn't want that to happen. If he could help the world find a solution for this problem, he would. "If I can make rain, no one will ever have to experience what he did."

The power of Conifer's simple words descended in every heart that heard them. He spoke truth from both his head and heart. His speech may not be as eloquent as he would have hoped but the words were his own, his gloriously original own words.

The judges sat stunned, not ready to proceed. Eventually each individual stood up, thanked Conifer, and firmly shook his hand before moving on to learn about static electricity. Anoop was still there and his mother would join them soon.

"Please know I didn't abandon you Conifer. I was always as near as your mother but wanted to let you have an opportunity to present the project on your own first. I planned to step in if you started to sink. You did outstanding, without my help."

"Until I almost started to rap about being happy and wanting my family with me. That would have been a disaster." Conifer hung his head.

"No, that would have been human and added another level of truth to your presentation. I have a good feeling about it, just wait and see." Anoop gave Conifer a mental pep talk.

Conifer's mom, not able to wait any longer, walked over to check on him. "So how do you feel like things went? What did the judges have to say? They had to think the cloud was pretty impressive at least." Brooke reached up and put her hand through the white manifestation still hovering above their heads.

"It is hard to tell. The judges were hard to read, but I think things went pretty well." Conifer spoke slowly without emotion.

There was a poignant pause as mother and son stared at each other both realizing what had just taken place. The science fair project may have gone well, but what happened moments afterward was profound. Conifer had spoken complete sentences without using song lyrics. Neither of them wanted to be the first to speak again and break the significance of the moment.

Tears formed in Brooke's eyes and her arms opened to receive her son. This was a day for firsts. Conifer stepped forward and into his mom's embrace. Had Anoop done something to his brain? Was there a blocked pathway he removed or a formula he patched in? Anoop still spoke mentally though Conifer no longer had to.

"You always had the ability to speak at any time, Conifer. It was not my doing."

"Then why now?" Conifer responded in kind.

"You just had to believe in yourself or maybe believe in something bigger than yourself." Anoop postulated. "When you stopped worrying about how to express yourself and began to care so deeply about helping others outside yourself, your words began to flow."

Brooke joined the conversation she could not hear with only one word. "How?"

"I guess I started to care about a bigger problem and mine washed away." Conifer replied.

Shortly before the end of the session, one of the judges stopped by Conifer's booth and attached a blue ribbon next to his poster board. Conifer and his cloud, who would hopefully both bring "Death to Drought" one day in the future, would definitely be going on to the state science fair later this spring. College was looking much more likely, along with possible scholarships. Anoop had healed a different kind of drought in Conifer's world.

Chapter 26 notes: Roughly 25 percent of people with autism speak few or no words. A generation ago, that figure was closer to 50 percent. Others may speak but have very limited language and communication skills. Hyperlexia, the ability to read above one's age or grade level in school commonly accompanies autism spectrum disorder. About 50,000 individuals with ASD will exit high school each year in the United States. Many services required by law end abruptly after high school. 35% of young adults with ASD do not have a job or receive postgraduate education after leaving high school. Individuals with ASD may be very creative. It is widely speculated that Albert Einstein, Isaac Newton, Andy Warhol, and Bill Gates are on the autism spectrum.

Conifer song lyrics- *Happy* by Pharrell Williams, *Don't Worry be Happy* by Bob Marley, and *We are Family* by Sister Sledge.

Chapter 27 – Paradise 2021

Anoop

"He led you through the great and terrible wilderness, with its fiery serpents and scorpions and thirsty ground where there was no water; He brought water for you out of the rock of flint." - Deuteronomy 8:15

Briary and Mehul were especially pleased with the outcome of Anoop's most recent assignment. "You mastered a way to give aid to an individual as well as the world simultaneously beta," Anoop's baba praised.

"My favorite part was how you were able to reach out to such a deserving member of our posterity when many others were not able to see him clearly. Grandpa John would be proud of your missionary skills in recovering a lost soul and helping him find his potential." Briary added.

"Guess I should have invited Grandpa John to toss on some religious insight. Maybe I can introduce him to Conifer another time," Anoop answered. He had worked on Conifer's temporal talents; his grandpa could help increase the understanding of his infinite soul. There were so many things about this realm that Anoop himself had yet to learn.

One of the most refreshing parts of this dimension was that everyone held the same status or was considered equal. There was no way to determine if a person had been a poor dirt farmer or a famous celebrity on earth. Glory and acclaim in paradise were based on what was in a person's heart. Those with the most love and charity exuded the most light but they were still not considered above another being. Anoop was pretty sure there were renown individuals in his midst, it was just that their accomplishments were weighed on a different scale here. The things that brought earthly fame did not guarantee a top place in the next world. In fact, fame may be a detriment causing a person to miss out on developing the things of their inner self that really mattered. Anoop was still unveiling it all, but it was a blessing to be able to have his parents near and be able to glean from their wisdom.

His wife Padma and each of their three children, as well as a few of his grandchildren, had arrived one at a time over the decades. Family connections were an important part of this culture. It would be hard to be 'heaven' without them. Anoop would look forward to welcoming his distant relative Conifer, but that bright boy still had much good to do in the world below before it would be his time to join this celestial habitat.

Dr. Strange would even be a part of this world one day. Most animals did not do as much good or as much bad as mankind. But the spirits of animals who had given their lives for the benefit of the world, whether in companionship or sacrificing themselves to be served on the table - their lives given to sustain another's - had a designated spot in paradise too. There were zoos on earth and even pet cafes in Japan to enjoy different species of animals. On a more massive scale, an area the size of a large continent was comprised of beasts who all lived in perfect harmony here in heaven. Anoop liked to stroll through their part of the kingdom and marvel at all the various creations wondering what kind of animal he would create if he ever got the opportunity.

Anoop was deep in his own thoughts when input from outside himself pushed its way in. "Do you miss earth?" He looked up to see his lovely Aashi beside him. Making sure he hadn't missed anything she had said to him, Anoop inquired, "What?"

"Do you miss earth? I wasn't there long enough to know what it is really like?"

Her wide eyes and deep sincerity touched his heart. "No, I don't miss earth but at times I wish I had a do-over.

Time there goes so fast and I worried too often about what was next, not about what was right in front of me. I had so many things that I wanted to accomplish that I didn't appreciate every day when I was living it."

"I would appreciate even one day there," Aashi sighed wistfully. "I would be so grateful for every, every minute."

Anoop beckoned the girl to his side, "Sit right here and ask me any and every question you have about living on earth and I will do my very best to make it come alive for you." Here he had been off helping others when someone right next to him needed him too. It appeared Anoop had not learned from his previous life not to miss what was going on in the present. "What would you like to know about first?"

"What does snow feel like?" Aashi asked with anticipation.

"Well, I may not be able to help you much there, we didn't have much snow in India, I know it is very cold. What do you have for me next?"

"How does it feel to lose someone you love when you are not sure you will see them again?"

Anoop wished he could go back to the question about snow, but he would do his best to let this daughter, who was hungry for a day on earth, experience it as best as he could from where they were right now.

Chapter 28- India 2023

Conifer/Juniper

*"But you can't start. Only a baby can start. You and me-
why, we're all that's been. The anger of the moment, the
thousand pictures, that's us. This land, this red land, is us;
and the flood years and the dust years and the
drought years are us."- John Steinbeck*

After twenty-two hours in flight, including a brief
layover in Guangzhou, China, the twins landed in Delhi.
Juniper had convinced their mother that if they were old
enough to go off to college on their own, they should be able
to handle a ten-day vacation. Juniper pointed out it would be
great practice in fending for themselves. And if Brooke went
with them, who would watch Dr. Strange? Brooke had
eventually granted her permission after both promised to text
her a minimum of four times a day. It was a small concession
for a non-chaperoned senior trip.

Juniper graduated from Bend High and Conifer from
Oak Leaf Academy only three days apart during the first week

of June. Now, only three weeks later, they were halfway around the world picking up pieces of their ancestral past. Conifer insisted that they had a relative named Anoop who had lived in India and since Juniper knew grandpa John had gone off to serve a mission there, she believed him. She was not sure how Conifer knew, but her brother said he had been in communication with the man. They were on a human treasure hunt to find the Sharma family and any remnants of the Fountains that may also remain in India, before heading off to their respective universities in the fall.

Oregon State University located in Corvallis over the Cascade mountain range only a few hours from Bend had offered Conifer a full scholarship. The college had outstanding science and agriculture departments, both of which were excited to work with Conifer. The feeling was mutual. Conifer was not going to end up institutionalized after all as Blaze had planned. Their father was currently AWOL. The man had disappeared off the face of the earth just like his ancestors, so Conifer's relocation was no longer a worry. Conifer hoped that his father knew how well he was doing, wherever he was.

Juniper decided to go to Willamette University in Salem, Oregon. The private liberal arts college had been founded in 1842 and was the oldest university in the Western

United States. Willamette offered Juniper a decent scholarship and the school was only forty-five minutes from OSU where Conifer would be, so they could see each other often. Stetson happened to be also attending college there. Not that that was the reason she chose to go to Willamette, but Juniper felt she did need to figure out if there was anything worth working towards between the two of them before she moved on. She knew she was still young but didn't want to lose what may be the best thing in her life merely because of independent woman pride. Growing up in her messed-up family had helped Juniper realize that life was best when relationships were healthy ones that made each half of the couple better people.

The Ridgeway siblings had booked a hotel for the night in Delhi before they joined up with a tour bus to Agra the next day. On the drive from the airport, the travel in Delhi was nothing like either Juniper or non-driver Conifer had ever seen. There were four lanes of traffic painted on the road, yet six lanes of cars squished into them with the vehicles nearly touching side to side. When Juniper voiced her concern to the taxi driver, he merely informed her that if the locals didn't pack in that close, no one would get to where they were going. The road was wall to wall cars and still moving. Maybe the U.S. could learn something about getting through traffic jams from these people.

A boy who appeared younger than ten years old was carrying a baby in his arms and maneuvering between the slow-moving cars, stopping to rest occasionally by sitting on a cement road divider as he begged for money. Other filthy, but smiling children reached out for offerings as the cars drove past. Juniper witnessed whole communities dwelling beside roadways with colorful clothes hanging out to dry and blankets spread out on dirt ground as they maneuvered past. An older man was napping on the cement barrier between the two directions of traffic. Brahma cattle, dogs, and even wild pigs wandered the busy streets. They had certainly landed in a different world. Juniper absorbing all of the colors, smells, and imagery hoped Conifer could process all the input without getting overwhelmed. She would watch him closely and help narrow his focus if needed.

After a hearty breakfast of rice, naan bread and vividly spiced sauces with some kind of meat mixed in, they boarded the tour bus to Agra. It was nice to be riding up high and not socked down amidst the traffic. A heavily accented English-speaking tour guide shared history and information about the sites they passed on the six-hour drive, which would have taken only four hours if Juniper was driving. These people were never in a hurry. Planted fields and dilapidated dwellings that looked like they had jumped out of another century dotted the drive. As they got closer to Agra, monkeys filled the trees and ran along the walls of an imposing fort.

The Ridgeways had planned to do a little sightseeing before seeking out their family roots. The main destination on this bus tour was one of the seven wonders of the world - the Taj Mahal. So, the two spent the rest of their day upon the famous monument's grounds. Conifer was more interested in the architecture and structure itself than in the romantic history of the tomb-palace. He was fascinated by the forward-thinking builders of the sixteenth century. Craftsmen who had the skills to enable a structure to survive through time. Two engineering feats especially stood out to him. First was that the Taj Mahal would have eroded years ago if the Yamuna River wasn't beside it. The foundation of Taj Mahal was made of timber using a pile technique, most foundations today were built with concrete which lasted much longer. The Taj Mahal's wooden base had been kept moist and strong by the waters of a river running beside it, thus exceeding expectations of its longevity. It sounded like even buildings needed water occasionally.

The other structural miracle was that the four kos minars or towers surrounding the Taj had been built tilted slightly outwards. In case of an earthquake or any other natural disaster, the minars would fall outwards keeping the main tomb safe from damage. Looking at the towers from any angle they still appeared straight. Conifer checked out this optical illusion from all four sides.

Juniper loved that the Taj Mahal changed its color at different times of the day depending on the light. Their guide told them that the color changed from a pinkish hue in the morning to milky white in the evening and appeared golden at night when the monument dome was lit by the moon. He informed them that some people think the unique feature of changing colors depicts the different moods of a woman, especially the mood of the emperor's queen buried there. Juniper laughed to herself that the palace or tomb was in reality just a huge mood ring.

As the sun set, the twins said goodbye to the tour group and took a tuk-tuk to their humble hotel. Both wondered what they would find tomorrow at the Sharma farm. Juniper had discovered more information on their John and Tristan Fountain relatives, but Conifer mysteriously had been able to uncover the location of a farm where Tristan's daughter had lived after marrying a local Sikh farmer. Briary Hope Fountain married Mehul Sharma and raised her family here in India just a few miles from Agra. This real-life story they were tracking was better than any novel to Juniper, and Conifer could hardly wait to see the place where his best friend in all eternity lived and called home while on earth.

Conifer could barely sleep. At dawn, he woke his sister ready to go. The farm was a few miles from town, too far to walk. After a bite to eat, they selected a few gifts as was customary to give their possible relatives and hailed a rickshaw. Luckily, the driver who stopped to pick them up spoke some English. Most locals spoke only Hindi unless they had been to school. Their relatives hopefully spoke both languages since a common grandparent had been British.

Conifer handed the address to the driver and he and Juniper climbed into the cart attached behind him. The sinewy man who appeared too small to bear their weight pedaled intently down the dusty country road. Sweat dripped down his neck and damped the back of his cotton shirt as the rickshaw was propelled with manual energy to carry the two Americans to their destination. Juniper felt a smidgen of guilt watching him strain but was glad they could give the man work. They arrived at the location Anoop had given Conifer before the sun was high in the sky. Juniper handed the driver a large tip before asking him to wait for them, or if he needed to go, to please return in an hour. The nameless man bobbed his head, grabbed the handlebars and scooted his rickshaw to the side of the home to wait in the shade.

The home standing before them was painted with bright orange paint that had begun to peel off in several spots. The original portion looked like it had been added upon a few times. One addition was olive green and another section mustard yellow. The windows were smaller than those back home. The glass in some was too cloudy to see through and others were covered from inside with a red busy-patterned fabric. Juniper took hold of Conifer's hand and with a deep breath knocked on the wooden door.

A slender man with a petite woman peering over his shoulder answered. They were both dressed in colors as vivid as those the house was painted in and the man wore a turquoise turban that covered his hair. The obvious question of 'why strangers were at their door' reflected on their faces.

Conifer was speaking quite well now but Juniper jumped in before he could, "Hello, we have traveled a long way, from the United States, and are looking for relatives of John Fountain."

Conifer found his voice and added, "And Anoop Sharma."

The couple looked at one another with slight concern before the man responded with, "Why would you like to find them?"

With relief that the homeowners did understand English Juniper continued, "We are related to these men and are looking for any family that we may have in India." Conifer again offered an addendum to his sister's words, "And Anoop is my friend."

The couple both smiled at the revelation, but the man took the conversational lead, "Anoop Sharma was my baba or father and my dada or grandfather was named that as well, so my baba was called Noopi by those who knew him. You were a friend of my father? He has passed away."

"I believe I am a friend of your grandfather," then realizing that may not be believable to those who knew that Anoop was buried many years ago, Conifer corrected, "He helped me with a project. Or his information did. So, I feel I know him."

"And our grandfather was John Fountain. I have been told you are related to him somehow too?" Juniper stuck with what was solid ground for her. She had seen records of a John Fountain.

"Won't you please come in and have tea with us and we can talk," the itsy-bitsy woman motioned them through her door.

The Ridgeway's were received into the Sharma's home as if they were family and then realized after digging around the family tree that indeed they were. John Fountain had been their common ancestor, his granddaughter Briary, was the elder Anoop's mother.

"Would you like to see where they are buried?" Mr. Sharma asked. "Not your direct relative John, he is buried at the mission. Most in India are cremated but great-grandma Briary started our family cemetery when she buried the young children she lost, and we have continued the tradition through the generations. Both Anoops are interned there."

Conifer sprung to his feet. "Yes. Please." Juniper was not sure if she should follow or stay with the current Mrs. Sharma but didn't want to miss anything. She followed her brother after remembering to say, "thank you for the tea," as they left.

The three took a path through the jowar plants and Anoop's grandson explained how they grew jowar and turmeric. This season their crop was doing well in comparison to dryer years. About three hundred yards from the house their guide stopped and pointed to a small plot of land dotted with wooden crosses and partial planks bearing the remnants of names.

Conifer felt he was on hallowed ground as he brushed dirt from the memorials looking for Anoop's name. He found Anoop's parents Briary and Mehul lying next to one another and partial names of other family members that he was not familiar with. Juniper stopped at Briary's grave feeling kinship there, while Conifer kept searching. The cemetery was quite small, it did not take Conifer long to recover Anoop Sharma. His friend had lived and died right here. Conifer was not crazy. Anoop had existed and still did elsewhere.

Conifer took out his phone and captured one of his first photos. He did not need a picture to remember this place, but it was nice to have hard evidence. A desire filled his head, not overwhelming it, but spreading a peaceful feeling throughout him. Conifer thought of the Taj Mahal and said aloud.

"I would like to provide a more permanent memorial for Anoop's gravesite if that is okay. And maybe some small cement markers or stone nameplates for each of the other plots, but a special one for Anoop if I can. I don't want him to be forgotten."

"We would be very grateful," the current keeper of the graveyard expressed.

Conifer knelt beside Anoop's beaten down mound and spoke mentally to his friend in case he was near, "Know you will never be washed away, even when the rains do come, but will always be remembered here in India until I meet you in paradise one day and can honor you there." Conifer pictured in his mind the simple, yet substantial stonework that would mark the unheralded life of a great man he now knew:

Anoop Sharma

1868 - 1948

Filled the world with living water…

Authors Notes

The idea for this book was given birth while walking over dry, parched earth on a hike and pondering the different definitions of drought. Realizing that droughts of the soul can be more devastating than those of the soil, I was intrigued by the dichotomy (or juxtaposition) of both. The story took root in my mind and needed to escape onto the page. I began by researching locations of great droughts throughout history and discovered that in the United States the Dust Bowl Famine of the 1930s with an estimated death toll of seven thousand was the only one substantial enough in the U.S. for my storyline and it was not early enough in history to work for my purposes.

The Great European Famine of the early 1300s which wiped out over five percent of the population was too long ago for the timeline and due to excessive rain, which caused crops to rot which is the opposite of my drought premise. (An interesting fact, the story of Hansel and Gretel likely originated during the European famine. Scholars speculate Hansel and Gretel's parents may have abandoned them as was common during this famine. In the first renditions of the story, the witch attempts to eat the children since she is starving.)

The other three countries that have been plagued by huge famines caused by drought are China, Africa, and India. My daughter and I had the pleasure to visit India in 2018. We were shown the wonders of the golden triangle by a tour guide named Anoop who was very humble, kind and extremely proud of his country. He shared much of the history and highlights of this area. India is a magical land of colors, flavors, and much poverty even today, 84% of India still did not have indoor toilets in 2016, but despite this, they remain open, warm, and a welcoming people. I decided to have my farming family dwell in the northern part of India that is rich with its history.

In recent centuries there have been three devastating famines that occurred in India. One of the deadliest famines in history, the Chalisa Famine of 1783, was triggered by El Niño weather patterns. It followed on the tracks of another famine the previous year and the combined famines spread throughout India greatly reducing the population. Roughly eleven million people died due to starvation or famine-related diseases.

About a hundred years later an intense drought led to widespread crop failure and resulted in the Great Famine of 1876. While food shortages caused by natural factors contributed to the famine, the British Empire exasperated its effects. The combination of minimal relief and heavy exportation made the famine one of the deadliest in Indian history with a death toll of five and a half million people. This is the famine that took place during my story. Anoop and his family weathered this drought disaster.

India's third famine was experienced twenty years later in north-central India and is mentioned briefly in Chapter 14. A chain of events began with a drought that occurred in 1895 due to a poor monsoon season which resulted in low crop yield and an initial famine. The government declared it a famine in 1896. However, the original drought added upon by another year of poor monsoons increased the famine's severity and spread it throughout India killing over a million of its people. While a heavy monsoon season in 1897 officially ended the famine, the heavy rains caused a malaria epidemic that was followed by an outbreak of the bubonic plague. Despite the famine officially ending in 1897, the effects of odd weather patterns lasted years.

While in modern times we still struggle with drought, hunger and natural disasters; the busy work-world bursting with modern technology and those seeking success at all costs, can bring upon an even more destructive drought of the soul. We have traded backbreaking labor of the body for exhaustion of the mind. While the advances of society have blessed our lives, we also miss out on many things that might bring peace. I was going to have chapter headings about autism (which has increased exponentially in the modern world) but did not want to signify in any way that it was a manifestation of drought. Conifer had much more to offer and give than his non-spectrum father.

The major analogy to take away from this story is that Anoop (named for water) not only helps bring that water to the world but also waters Conifer's (named after a tree) soul and helps him to grow and become the mature man that he was destined to be. Anoop was a surrogate father to Conifer since the father that Conifer was born to, nurtured his son's roots with nothing but drought.

P.S. This book was completed before the worldwide COVID 19 pandemic during 2020 occurred. I considered modifying the storyline to include the presence of the virus but decided readers would realize this was a work of fiction and not an actual account of the time period.

Acknowledgments

There are always so many factors that go into the birthing of a book. Chelsea, thank you for trekking to India with me and for painting this perfect cover. And real Anoop (wherever you are) thank you for opening my eyes to the magic, beauty, and story of your unique country. Jill and Derek thank you for introducing me to my first autistic experience and for making sure my portrayal of Conifer rang true. Stephanie, Keegan, Teri, Sandy and the original Briary thank you for reading various drafts of *Drought* as the story came to life. Then, of course, I am always grateful to any readers who take the time to open this book and go on the journey with my newly created friends. Your actions bring Anoop, Conifer, Juniper and their parents to life over and over again.

Discussion Questions

1) Do you believe that a drought of the *soil* which causes many people to die of famine or a drought of the human *soul* that affects the lives of those nearest him/her is more devastating?

2) Do you believe that people here on earth are supported or even inspired by those who have gone before and now live on the other side of the veil? When did you realize Anoop was Neem?

3) Do you know anyone on the autism spectrum? What gifts do they have that others may not see or be aware of?

4) Did you prefer the modern-day Ridgeway family storyline or the one of the Sharma family living a century ago in India? Which character did you relate to or enjoy the most?

5) How did the marriages of Briary/Mehul vs. Brooke/Blaze differ? Did Briary and Mehul give up too much to marry outside of their religious beliefs? Do you think Brooke could have or should have been a better wife to Blaze? Is the most important part of marriage supporting a spouse to become the best version of themselves?

6) Discuss what part *Matilda* the musical and Dr. Strange played in the story. Can theater or the arts bring about positive changes in people that are struggling or closed off? How about animals, can they play a part in healing a broken soul?

7) Did Conifer speaking in song lyrics seem believable? Why or why not? What song would you have liked him to speak or rap?

8) Have you ever researched your own genealogy? Do you think our ancestors play a part in who we are today?

9) Do you know anyone you think could be a psychopath? Do you think Blaze was one or was he just a product of his own background? Is nurture or nature more important in character development?

10) Do you hope Juniper and Stetson end up together somewhere in the future or were they just a first romance or first loves? What else would you like to see happen as the story continues?

Works Cited:

https://www.ranker.com/list/the-worst-droughts-and-famines-in-history/drake-bird?ref=search

https://www.funeralwise.com/customs/hindu/

https://en.wikipedia.org/wiki/Hinduism_and_Sikhism

https://en.wikipedia.org/wiki/William_Carey_(missionary)

https://www.bustle.com/p/10-song-lyrics-about-school-for-back-to-school-2018-instagram-captions-10193517

https://www.history.com/topics/india/taj-majal

https://www.kidzone.ws/plants/trees.htm

https://www.sharefaith.com/blog/2013/08/top-10-popular-hymns-time-history/

https://www.investopedia.com/articles/investing/022716/5-best-performing-stocks-last-20-years-gmcr-celg.asp

https://www.quora.com/Who-is-Doctor-Strange-and-what-are-his-superpowers

https://weatherstreet.com/weatherquestions/What_is_cloud_seeding.htm

http://www.playbill.com/article/new-study-finds-theatre-can-help-children-on-autism-spectrum-com-365305

https://allthatsinteresting.com/indoor-clouds

https://cloudappreciationsociety.org/berndnaut-smilde-making-clouds/

https://themighty.com/2016/07/what-autism-meltdowns-feel-like-for-autistic-people/

https://www.usbr.gov/mp/arwec/water-facts-ww-water-sup.html

https://www.massgeneral.org/children/autism/lurie-center/30-facts-to-know-about-autism-spectrum-disorder

Conifer's Songs:

Mad World, by Roland Orzabal

Banana Pancakes, by Jack Johnson

Get Outta My Dreams, Get into My Car, by Billy Ocean

On the Road Again, by Willie Nelson

Life is a Highway, by Tom Cochran

On my Own, by Samantha Barks

Hound Dog, by Elvis Presley

I Love my Dog, by Cat Stevens

Little Boys Grow Up and Dogs get Old, by Luke Bryant

Tell Her No by The Zombies

Stay by Rihanna

The Show Must Go On by Three Dog Night

A Whole New World by Jodi Benson

Thriller by Michael Jackson

Bring Him Home by Colm Wilkinson

Angel by Sara McLachlan

Happy by Pharrell Williams

Don't Worry be Happy by Bob Marley

We are Family by Sister Sledge.

About the Author

Teresa Meyerhoeffer Christensen has experienced all the elements of romance, drama, comedy, intrigue, tragedy, and adventure in over a half-century of earth living. She was born in Idaho to a basketball-playing, college president father, and cheerleader mother, who taught her to love to learn. She married her high school sweetheart, graduated as an RN, survived cancer, raised six amazingly unique children, taught religion classes for many years, was elected to the Bend-Lapine School Board while living in Oregon and has served on various other boards in many volunteer positions. She now lives at over five thousand feet in Mountain Green where the air, as well as the veil between heaven and earth, are both much thinner and the inspiration is plentiful. Teresa finally has the time to put down on page all of the stories that have been roaming around in her head for years. *Drought* is Teresa's sixth book. William Shakespeare was her twelfth great uncle. Website: www.TeresaMeyerhoefferChristensen.com